# Six Degrees of Death

## by

## Marian Exall

The Wild Rose Press, Inc.
PO Box 708
Adams Basin, NY 14410-0708
Visit us at www.thewildrosepress.com

Publishing History
First Edition, 2024
Trade Paperback ISBN 978-1-5092-5886-4
Digital ISBN 978-1-5092-5887-1

*Previously Self-Published Kindle 2021*
Published in the United States of America

## Dedication

To Pen Ultimate, my critique group. They love a good mystery!

**Also by this author and published by The Wild Rose Press, Inc.**

*Daughters of* Riga

Chapter 1

"Students! I hate them!" Geraldine looked at Thomas to make sure she had her husband's attention before she started reading aloud the latest grammatical idiocy in the essay she was grading. He was sprawled on the sofa, pretending to read last Sunday's *New York Times*. Confronted with a raised newspaper and unwilling to take silence as assent, she sighed and went back to her silent review.

Behind the newsprint shield, Thomas clenched his jaw. *Why teach if you hate students? Why involve me in your never-ending condescending critique of their writing skills?* His wife had a tenured position and a comfortable income. Unlike him, she didn't have to put up with editors mauling his articles, telling him his style was too pedantic, cutting 2,000 words down to nine hundred, "blog-length" for God's sake. And that was when an article was accepted for publication, which hadn't happened for months. "Freelance journalist"— how he insisted Geraldine introduce him at faculty parties—had meant "unemployed hack" for a long time now. Thomas knew his foul mood had its root in another literary agent's rejection—the twenty-ninth but who's counting—of his novel, "a sprawling saga set in an elite Long Island community…an autocratic patriarch…the sensitive younger son, a writer…tragic death of the only woman who understood…" The blurb virtually wrote itself. All it needed was a few laudatory words by a best-selling author, a literary prizewinner. But who could he approach? More to the point, who would respond to his approach? At this rate, Thomas would be dead before his *magnum opus* saw the light of day.

He hadn't told Geraldine about the rejection, or that he had been querying agents about the novel at all. He couldn't stand her cloying sympathy. Or her useless advice. "Why don't you ask Betsy Pinero for a referral to her agent? Or I could get Professor Hersch to make a recommendation?" He shuddered at the thought of Women's Studies Betsy, author of a best-selling exposé of sexual harassment in the fitness industry, or Hersch, the octogenarian chair of the English department, looking at his work.

A sudden intake of breath from Geraldine, precursor to another diatribe against poor student writing, recalled him to the moment. He was about to announce that he was going for a walk when his phone rang. *Saved by the bell.*

"I'm going to have to take this," Thomas said, frowning. He stood and hurried through the kitchen and out the back door before accepting the call.

"Yes?" The caller was named on the screen as Hannah P. He had no reason to keep her identity a secret from Geraldine. Hannah was Geraldine's friend as well, and a member of their book club, but he wasn't in the mood for sharing even inconsequential information.

"Hi, it's me."

Thomas detested this casual way of initiating a conversation.

"Who's speaking?"

"You know perfectly well. It's Hannah! I'm calling

about book club. You and Gerry are coming, right?"

"Well, it's still a week off; I haven't really checked—"

"You absolutely must be there. You've read the book?" He hadn't. He knew Geraldine had bought a copy and it was prominent on her nightstand. On other occasions, when he hadn't been able to find time to finish a selection, Geraldine had given him a synopsis, and his general knowledge of literature would allow him to wing it. Fortunately, Hannah rushed on without waiting for his response.

"Great news! Kwendi Barbera is coming to our book club!" An expectant pause. "You know, the author. It turns out he knows my daughter, they do kickboxing together, and she's persuaded him to come to our meeting. Isn't that great?" There was the sound of a scuffle and a crash from the other end of the phone. "Uh-oh. Have to go. Jeremy's found the *carne asada*. See you both next Tuesday." Click. *Saved by the click.*

****

"Jeremy, you bad, bad dog!" Hannah threw her phone down and chased the miniature dachshund out the French doors onto the patio. Jeremy hadn't consumed much of the spicy pulled pork she had slow-cooked all day for a Mexican supper, but knowing where his snout had been previously, she thought it would probably be best to empty the rest into the garbage. She wanted the meal to be special. Dave, her lover, was coming over. *My lover.* She lingered over the words. It had been a long dry season before Dave showed up. He was a long-haul semi driver with a graying-blond ponytail and muscles everywhere. Well, a bit of a beer belly too perhaps, but that was to be expected after age forty and in a sedentary

3

job. They had met at a gas station when he had literally saved her life, changing a flat tire on her car at eleven o'clock at night. The gas station attendant was distinctly unhelpful, especially considering it must have been broken glass in the station forecourt *he* had failed to sweep up which had caused the puncture.

Hannah wasn't quite ready to introduce Dave to her friends yet. She wasn't a snob, but she suspected some of them were. Dave just needed a little "polishing." She knew he had a fascinating back story, if only she could persuade him to share it. He was a working-class hero, she was certain. Perhaps tonight when she introduced him to Aubrey, her daughter, he would open up about his past. Aubrey was such a free spirit, no inhibitions, and she had such interesting friends. Her language was a bit crude—effing this and effing that—but all young people spoke that way nowadays. It showed they weren't intimidated by authority, that they were passionate and committed. Hannah loved that.

She would call Aubrey and get her to pick something up from the deli on her way home. At the same time, she could warn Aubrey that Dave was coming over for dinner. Aubrey didn't know Hannah had a boyfriend—*a lover*—and she wouldn't want to be blindsided. Now, where was her phone?

\*\*\*\*

Aubrey had just rappelled down the 5.10 climb, the toughest at the gym, and was dripping sweat when her phone buzzed. She grabbed it out of her climbing bag with chalky hands and checked the screen. With a hiss between her teeth, she cut off the call and threw the device back into the bag.

"Bad news?" Cindy was twice her age and twice as

fit. Scrawny thin but strong as cured leather, Cindy had led the climb up, setting a fast pace.

"Just my fucking mother. It's bad enough I have to crash at her place, but now she wants to be part of my life, too." Aubrey put air quotes around "part of my life" and pulled a face. Cindy laughed.

"So glad I never had kids. They might have turned out like you!" She play-punched Aubrey on the shoulder. Even for a play-punch, it stung. "Let's get a beer."

**** 

By eight p.m. Geraldine had finished her first read-through of the Intro to Literature term papers, and she was exhausted. She had made notes on a separate pad, knowing that her first acerbic reactions would need to be sweetened before she committed them to the margins of the students' work. It was after all a freshman class. A minority of these students would persevere to hone their writing skills and refine their analyses, and she didn't want to stifle their enthusiasm at this early stage. It was so easy to mistake cynicism for sophistication, and to be impressed by jaded critics who had given up on producing anything original themselves. She thought of Thomas, what sharp and lucid prose he had turned out when he was younger, before he had stopped being a reporter and started calling himself a journalist.

She wondered who had called earlier. Thomas kept secrets from her, she was aware. He needed them to maintain the mystique that he had important projects in hand, that he was not just a house husband, financially dependent on her. Lately, however, his benign little subterfuges had taken on a more conspiratorial aspect. He'd disappear into his study, emerging in a dark mood that persisted all evening. Perhaps she could cheer him up tonight by making his favorite *pasta carbonara* for supper. She'd open a bottle of red and tell him about the first-year student who thought the Brontë sisters' problem was their corsets were laced too tight. After all, she had her own secrets to protect.

Chapter 2

Dave took an Uber back to the distribution center where the rig was being loaded. He was tempted to tell the driver to pull over at a bar. He needed a strong drink after the shitty evening at Hannah's, but DOT regs allowed him to start driving again at 2 a.m. and he wanted to get going. He couldn't risk losing his license to a random alcohol test.

God! The daughter was a bitch! Amber—Audrey—something like that. She barely said a word to him, just glared with those mean little eyes. If *his* daughter treated her mother like that, she'd feel the back of his hand. Emma was only five but already knew how to say "ma'am" and "sir" to adults, and "please" and "thank you" at the dinner table. Thoughts of Emma brought his wife Joanne to mind, and guilt washed over him again. He had planned to let Hannah down gently this evening, tell her he was married with a family, and although Hannah was a great person and all, he just couldn't see her again. But with the daughter there, he hadn't been able to talk to her. Hannah obviously expected him to stay the night, but he'd used the schedule as his excuse.

"Nah, gotta roll out tonight, or I won't make it back to St. Louis on time."

"But you've hardly eaten a thing!" Hannah had piled his plate with something she called taco casserole. It looked like the dog's dinner.

"Yeah, not a big fan of Mexican food. It upsets my gut."

The daughter let out a disgusted sound, and stood up. He thought this might be his chance to talk to Hannah, but Amber/Audrey just plopped herself down on the sofa and started playing with her phone.

"Well, at least let me pack this up for you to take with you. You might get hungry later."

So here he sat in the back of a Toyota with a plastic container full of orange mess on his lap, and an ache in his heart for home. The ride dropped him outside the industrial area on the waterfront where the distribution center was located. He turned his collar up against the November drizzle and looked around for a place to dump the container. A homeless guy was curled up in the shelter of a bus stop.

"Here. You hungry?" Dave extended the plastic box toward the man's back. The man slowly sat up and stared at Dave. He had black stringy hair and a sparse beard. His face was so thin that his eyes seemed enormous.

"Here, you can have this," Dave repeated, pushing the food forward. Perhaps the guy didn't speak English; he looked Latino, so maybe he liked Mexican food. Slowly, as if to a rabid dog, a hand reached out to take the plastic box.

"Enjoy!" Dave called back as he hurried away.

As soon as he climbed into the semi's cab, he called Joanne. Just hearing her sleepy hello eased the tension from his body.

"Hi, sweetheart. What's up?"

"What do you think is up? It's nearly midnight here."

"Aw, I'm sorry. Did I wake you?"

"No, I thought you'd call. I'm watching reruns of *Parks and Rec* in bed."

"Stay right there. I'm on my way."

Joanne chuckled. They talked for a while about the kids, Joanne's mother who was sick again, what time he'd be home on Wednesday. They fell silent, and Dave thought briefly of admitting the Hannah thing. Would Joanne believe it was just a pity fuck? Hannah had seemed so needy and pathetic, standing in the rain next to her disabled car. After he'd changed the tire, he'd followed her home to make sure the spare didn't fail. It looked pretty sketchy. When she'd invited him in for a drink, he accepted out of politeness. Then she came on to him. What was a guy to do? It seemed rude to walk out. But would Joanne see that? Did women even get the pity fuck idea?

The moment passed and they said their goodbyes and love you's and ended the call.

****

Cindy volunteered every Monday night at the Mission. She'd been doing it for about a year, 8 p.m. to 8 a.m., arriving in time to help clear up after the meal, then hanging out with the guests until lights out at 10 p.m. Cindy was a good listener. The men accepted her presence. With her androgynous physique and grungy athletic clothes, she fit in where other "do-gooder" volunteers were ignored or avoided.

The shelter had fifty beds for men, arranged in two dormitories. They were supposed to sign in for the night before dinner was served at 6:00, but the doors weren't locked and there was always someone wandering outside later for a smoke, to meet a lady friend or maybe to score drugs. Tonight the weather kept everyone inside. After lights out, the volunteers sat in the office with the staff member on duty. They drank coffee, read and dozed, or reviewed the protocols for all conceivable emergencies that were posted around the walls. Tonight, it was just Cindy and Marco, the Mission employee on nights this week. In spite of his youth and improbable good looks, Marco seemed to have earned the respect of the men who came to the shelter. Like Cindy, he was a good listener. And he was a hard worker, not afraid of the grittier tasks associated with keeping the place operating smoothly.

Cindy was deep into a science fiction novel when Marco spoke.

"Hear that? Sounds like someone's throwing up."

Cindy listened. The noise from the communal restroom that served Dormitory A was unmistakable.

"I'll go see what's happening." Marco got up and Cindy followed him out of the office, then waited in the hallway. After a few moments, Marco came back, guiding a thin dark man who was hunched over and gripping his stomach.

"I'll clean up in there. You look after our friend. Take him out to reception. Better take a bucket."

Cindy nodded. After stopping at the utility closet, she steered the man out into the reception area. His arm under her hand felt frail like bird's bones. The smell of vomit on his washed-out sweatshirt made her want to gag, but she kept close to his side until he sat on one of the benches lining the lobby. Having placed the bucket on the floor between the man's feet, she went into the small bathroom that served the reception and office area, wrung out some disposable towels in cold water, and filled a paper cup.

"Here, rinse out your mouth with water. You'll feel

better." Cindy still hadn't glimpsed the man's face, which he kept bent over the bucket, curtains of greasy hair falling forward. He took a sip but immediately started retching. She waited until he had finished, then placed a damp paper towel on the back of his neck, and started gently cleaning his hands with another.

"Sorry." The man's voice was a cracked whisper, his face still hidden.

"It's okay. When you feel better, take off your shirt. I'll go find you a clean one." There was a supply of fresh clothes in the utility closet for emergencies like this. She returned with a blue sweatshirt with U Cal Berkeley emblazoned in yellow on the chest. The colors looked startlingly bright in the fluorescent light of the reception area.

The man was still hunched over the bucket. Perhaps he was embarrassed to bare his torso in front of her.

"Look, I'll leave it here, then get some more water and towels." She placed the shirt on the bench next to him and retreated into the bathroom, taking the bucket with her to empty and swill out. When she came out, he had changed shirts and made an attempt to clean himself up, wiping off his face and hair with the damp towels. His face was haggard, sunken cheeks and huge luminous black eyes. Cindy wondered if he was on something.

"What's your name? I'm Cindy." Silence, but he kept eye contact. Perhaps he didn't speak English. Cindy had never seen him at the shelter before and didn't remember him from earlier that evening when she had wandered around the dining room.

"I'm Cindy," she said pointing to her own chest. "And you…?" She pointed to him.

"Hay Zoos." Cindy puzzled over his response, until

she realized what he was saying. *Jesús*. She spoke a little Spanish and tried it out now. "*Còmo estas? Mejor?*"

"*Si.*" The man—Jesús—smiled, transforming the ravaged face for a moment and, with the long hair and beard, making Cindy think of another Jesus in religious icons she had seen in European churches. She continued in her makeshift Spanish.

"You eat dinner here?" She knew Marco would need this information. If it had been the shelter meal that made Jesús sick, they could expect an epidemic of vomiting and would need to call in reinforcements.

"No, not here. A man, stranger, give the dinner." He waved his hand vaguely toward the door to indicate the outside. "You want me to go now?"

"No! You can stay, of course. Rest. Sleep." She gestured at the bench. Obediently, Jesús stretched out on the bench and closed his eyes. Cindy made another trip to the utility closet for a couple of blankets and some threadbare towels. She rolled up a towel and offered it to Jesús as a pillow. Then she spread a blanket over him. His eyes were closed and soon his breathing became deep and even. Cindy knew she should go back to the office and check in with Marco, but she felt the urge to stay and watch over Jesús. So instead she made her own bed on the bench opposite, and turned out the lights. In the glow from the streetlights outside, she watched the man as he slept.

She wondered where Jesús came from and how he had ended up at the Mission. His hands, although dirty with ragged nails, were not calloused or scarred by work. Not the hands of someone who worked construction or in the fields. The sweatshirt was too big for him; the neck gaped. Cindy saw something glint in the hollow of his collarbone. She got up quietly and crept closer. On a thin leather thong around his throat hung a simple cross. The metal was a dull gray and scratched into the center was a symbol, a triangle containing a circle. She had seen the symbol before somewhere, but couldn't remember where. She went back to the other bench and lay down. She listened to the rhythm of Jesús' breathing and adjusted her own breath to keep the same steady pace. Soon she was asleep.

****

Marco finished cleaning up the mess in the Dormitory A bathroom, checked the other dormitory, and, satisfied that no one else was throwing up, returned to the office. He picked up the book he was reading for a college class—Dickens' *Bleak House*—but found his mind wandering. After five minutes, when Cindy still hadn't returned, he went down the corridor to the reception area. The lights had been turned out, but he could make out the humps on the two benches facing each other. He thought of the rules and procedures posted on the office wall: *After lights out, lock the front door, but leave the light on in the reception area,* and *Volunteers should remain in the office with on-duty staff after lights out, unless required to deal with an emergency under the direction of staff.* He should wake Cindy and tell her to go back to the office; he should turn on the lights and double-check the front door was still locked. Yeah, right. Cindy was sensible and mature; he wouldn't have sent her to handle the sick guy on her own otherwise. If he turned on the lights, both sleepers would wake up, and the poor dude probably needed to rest up away from the background rumble of coughs and snores in the dormitories. Anyway, whatever he had might be infectious, so it was best to keep him separate.

Marco tiptoed back to the office, grinning to himself. The truth was the two sleepers looked so peaceful and somehow innocent he couldn't bring himself to disturb them. Peace and innocence: two words not often associated with a homeless shelter in the city. He thought back to the time he'd been homeless. A gradual slide from a shared apartment to friends' couches, a few weeks living in his car, and then the sudden plunge to sleeping in doorways, being rousted by the police, then wandering the streets in the pre-dawn hours looking to score. His arrest for shoplifting and incarceration in the overcrowded county jail would have been the start of an even steeper decline except for a sympathetic judge in Drug Court and a caseworker who said she believed in him. At twenty-seven, nine months sober, he wasn't going to waste his second chance. Taking the job at the Mission was part of his court-mandated recovery program: he needed that repeated reminder of how easy it would be to lose everything again. Besides, the night shifts fitted well with his college schedule and gave him plenty of time to study.

This was his second chance at higher education, too. He'd dropped out after a single semester the first time, unprepared for the freedom of living away from home, and the temptations of booze and drugs after an evangelical upbringing in a rural community. He wanted to major in something practical like Business or Computer Science, but he had to get some foundation courses out of the way first. Intro to Literature appeared an easy option for fulfilling his English requirement. He'd enjoyed stories as a child. But these texts were *long*, man.

14

Marco picked up *Bleak House* again and flicked to the back. Only 818 pages. Christ. He sighed and found his place on page 71. This Skimpole character: Marco recognized him. There was always someone like that around the dives he used to hang out at, playing the innocent victim, expecting you to help him out, even if you were flat broke. And Richard's an idiot; you could tell he's bad news for Esther, even this early in the story. Marco made it to the end of the chapter before his mind wandered again.

Professor Harmon—Geraldine Harmon, it said in the course catalog—was a good teacher. She filled in the context—details about the author's life and times—and connected them to contemporary themes. She subtly drew students into class discussions, and didn't ridicule their opinions. Even so, Marco dreaded being called on. He didn't fear appearing a fool in front of his classmates. From his perspective—older and with a bleaker life experience—most of them were spoiled children anyway. But he had decoded Professor Harmon's mannerisms—the tight smile, almost a grimace, unsuccessfully hidden by a quick turn toward the whiteboard at the front of the class, whenever someone ventured a stupid comment, or, worse, admitted they had nothing to say. He was afraid of disappointing her. And he knew even if he read all night, he'd never complete the assignment. Turning over his feelings, he concluded Professor Harmon was a mother figure. He had never succeeded in meeting his own mother's narrow standards which relied on the threat of hellfire and damnation awaiting any deviation. Now he was seeking a kinder, gentler substitute. But the irrational dread of falling into the fiery pit persisted. His case worker's voice echoed in his brain: *confront your fears, admit your vulnerability!* Yeah, that all sounded fine in group sessions during rehab, but out in the real world…

Harmon had office hours at 10 a.m. the next day. If he skipped the nap he'd promised himself before his noon class, he could go talk to her about his difficulties. Not whining, not asking for special treatment, just explaining he was a slow reader, that sometimes the words jumped around, and he had to go back and re-read the paragraph before he understood it. Perhaps she had some tips, or maybe an audio version of the text?

Two a.m. Three hours until he had to start the coffee brewing. He abandoned Dickens and stretched out on the sofa.

Chapter 3

Marco was bummed to see another student already waiting when he arrived outside Professor Harmon's office at five minutes to ten.

"She's not in," the girl said, without looking up from her phone. He recognized her from the class but didn't remember her name, if he had ever known it. She wore ripped jeans and an army surplus jacket, standard college uniform whether your parents were billionaires or street people. Short jet-black hair with a purple streak, plenty of ear and eyebrow piercings, but not nose, lips or tongue—at least that he could see. No tats showing either. So, middle-class, playing at rebellion.

"Okay." He leaned against the wall opposite her and practiced his centering breathing.

"You're in Intro to Literature." It was a statement, not a question. She scrolled her eyes up and down him. Perhaps her phone battery had died—he couldn't think why else he had inspired her interest.

"Mmm. My name's Marco."

"Aubrey. So, you dropping out too?"

"What? No! Why would I drop out of the class?"

Aubrey shrugged. "Because it's a fucking drag. Tomorrow's the deadline for switching to auditing. That way, you avoid a fail or incomplete. Next semester, there's a T.A. teaching Twentieth Century Lit. I know him." She grinned slyly. "He'll give you a B for just showing up occasionally."

"Interesting," Marco responded coolly. Definitely middle-class: let mommy and daddy burn through the tuition payments for a few more years while she partied.

It was now five after. Marco walked past the girl to knock on the professor's door.

"Told you. Not there." Aubrey was back hunched over her phone. Marco ignored her, took out his own phone, and dialed the English Department number. He heard a distant ringing, then a voice answered.

"English Department, Anne Summers speaking."

"Hi, Anne. I thought Professor Harmon had office hours today at ten, but she doesn't appear to be in her office."

"No, she's there. She's been in since before nine. I would have seen her if she'd left. Just knock and go in."

Marco thanked her and disconnected. He pointed to the door.

"Aubrey? You were here first. The secretary says to go on in."

Aubrey shrugged, her favorite gesture. "Nah, it's cool. You go first."

Marco rapped, waited a few seconds, then entered. Professor Harmon had fallen forward, her hands stretched out over her head, the fingers clawed on the polished wood of the desk. Marco rushed forward, calling her name. She didn't move. After a brief hesitation, he pushed her hair aside to feel for a pulse in the neck. The skin was cold and clammy. He looked up and saw Aubrey standing in the doorway, her mouth hanging open.

"Call for medical help. Now!"

Aubrey took a few beats to react. It didn't matter.

The professor was dead.

****

Thomas Harmon performed domestic chores with precision and efficiency. He vacuumed the carpets in straight lines like a Wimbledon lawn tennis court. Geraldine said it was a shame to mess them up by walking on them. He prided himself on never running the dishwasher until it was full, organized according to scientific principles that ensured every utensil emerged clean.

Having completed these two tasks, Thomas started to prepare his midmorning coffee. His phone rang while he was adding freshly ground coffee to the apparatus—a critical point in the espresso coffee-making ritual. He was tempted to ignore the insistent sound. *If it's important they'll leave a voicemail.* But then he thought that this might be *the* call: the agent blown away by his first thirty pages and wanting more. Or at least an editor in need of a puff piece to fill a gap in January's *Northwest Retirement News.* He turned off the kettle, and picked up the device.

"Mr. Harmon? I'm going to connect you to Professor Hersch now. Please hold."

If Thomas wasn't so irritated, he would laugh: the old man still had to have his secretary place his calls. He probably didn't know how to turn an iPhone on. Probably didn't have one.

"Harmon? Thomas? I'm afraid I have some serious news." There was a pause, then *sotto voce,* "Is this thing on?"

"Yes, Professor, I can hear you." Thomas regretted answering the call. No doubt the news was serious in the solipsistic world of the English Department at a second-rate college, but why was the Department Chair calling to tell *him* about it?

"It's about Professor Harmon…Geraldine…your wife."

*Yes, I know she's my wife.* He wondered what she'd done now. Been caught *in flagrante* with a sophomore in her *Beowolf* seminar? Unlikely. Geraldine's passions were confined to literature; sex had become an infrequent occurrence. Perhaps she'd leaked the exam questions to her favorite student? More likely, still not probable. The ancient professor continued to waffle on, and Thomas lost the thread for a moment. He could smell the coffee waiting on the counter for the addition of boiling water.

"…dead."

"What?" *Who's dead? Why is he telling me?* Something caught in his throat, and his attempt to speak came out as a gasp.

"I'm so very sorry. It must have been her heart. She will be sorely missed. I expect the…um…authorities will be in touch about the…er…when they determine…" Professor Hersch, at a loss for words, stopped speaking. As he did so, the front doorbell rang.

Thomas cast his eyes around the kitchen, looking for something to latch on to, some clue that this was a bad dream. The doorbell would then resolve into the morning alarm, and he would wake up to see Geraldine's head on the pillow next to him. The two-note "ding-dong" repeated from the front of the house.

"I have to go," Thomas muttered into the phone, and put the cell phone down, leaving the diminishing sound of Professor Hersch reciting platitudes into an empty kitchen. Thomas was so numbed by the call that he opened the front door without checking the identity of his visitor through the peephole as he usually did. Hannah rushed over the threshold and enveloped him in an enthusiastic embrace.

"Oh, you poor man! You poor, poor man!"

Thomas held his arms stiff at his sides. He could smell Hannah's pungent perfume, something musky and rich. And something else: marijuana! He thought he might be sick; he tried to stop breathing.

After a few seconds, Hannah released him and took a step back. Thomas gulped a mouthful of fresh air, provoking another "Oh, you poor man!" from Hannah. Numbness was replaced by anger. He could feel it rising up from his chest, suffusing his face with molten rage, filling his mouth with useless, wordless fury.

"How did you…? What?" he croaked.

"Aubrey texted me from school. It was she who found the body—I mean Gerry—and I came straight over. I couldn't bear to think of you being alone at a moment like this!" She took his arm and, ignoring his resistance, steered him into the living room. "What you need is a stiff drink. Just sit down and let me look after you. I'm here for you, Tommy."

She pushed him into a seated position on the sofa, then walked over to the drinks tray on the side console, selected a bottle, and poured hefty slugs into two tumblers.

"Here you are. I know you don't drink in the morning, but this is medicinal." She sat down next to him, turning to examine his profile. "Shock. That's what it is. Just take deep breaths and sip on this." She demonstrated by taking a swallow from her glass.

Whiskey. He hated whiskey. It was Geraldine's

21

drink. *Just wait until she comes home and sees—* He put the glass down hard on the coffee table in front of him. Hannah had already half-finished her drink. He had to make her go away this very moment or he would kill her. With an extreme effort to control his anger, he spoke through gritted teeth.

"I'd like to be alone now. I have things to do, calls to make. Just…go!"

"Oh, no, honey! That can all wait. I'm going to stay and help you through this." Hannah edged closer along the sofa, placing a hand on his. He withdrew from her touch just as the doorbell sounded again. *Jesus, what is this? A frat party?* At least he had an excuse to stand up and move away from Hannah.

"No, let me deal with this." Hannah pulled him back down, and stood up herself. He pursued her to the door, jockeying to get there first.

"Oh, it's the police," Hannah said, as she swung the door wide.

Two uniformed cops stood on the front porch, an older male and a younger female. The older male spoke past Hannah to Thomas.

"Mr. Harmon? May we come in? We have some bad news, I'm afraid." They gave their names, which Thomas instantly forgot.

"Yes. My wife. I know," Thomas said, calmer now and relieved not to be alone with Hannah. He returned to the sitting room, trailed by the police, leaving Hannah to shut the door.

"And you are?" The female cop turned to Hannah with an inquiring tilt of the head.

"I'm a close friend," she laughed self-consciously. "Of *both* the Harmons. Well, obviously not Gerry's now, because…" She pulled her shoulders back. "Hannah Peters. I'm here to support Tommy. I came over as soon as I heard."

"Perhaps you might like to make some tea?" The policewoman looked from the untouched glass of whiskey in front of Thomas to the empty one in Hannah's hand. "If it's not too much trouble? We'd like to speak to Mr. Harmon for a few minutes."

Hannah gave a tight smile and took herself off to the kitchen, closing the door with firmness just short of a slam.

The older cop took over the lead.

"I'm very sorry to have to tell you that your wife was found dead in her office at the college shortly after ten this morning." He seemed tired, moving through the motions of a familiar protocol. His young colleague was more alert, looking around the room, squinting to read the titles on the bookcase, and thumbing the pages of her notebook, as if eager to record something in it.

"Did your wife have any underlying medical conditions?" the policeman continued.

"No. She's in perfect health. What are you suggesting? A heart attack?"

Thomas's question was ignored.

"When did you last see Mrs. Harmon?"

"Professor Harmon," Thomas corrected. "This morning. We had breakfast together, just as we always do. Everything was fine." Except they'd had a flaming row, Geraldine declaring she could no longer bear to live with him, accusing him of self-centeredness, self-indulgence, self-aggrandizement. "Self, self, self, that's all you ever think of!" Remembering her words now, Thomas felt his fury begin to reignite, but he knew he must retain his self-control. He suppressed a twisted smile at the irony: self again.

The change of facial expression did not escape the young policewoman.

"Yes? Your wife was well? Everything normal?"

"Yes! Now please tell me about Geraldine. How did she die? Are you certain it's her? Hannah said her daughter found her. What was Aubrey doing there? It all seems unbelievable."

The male cop made a calming gesture with his hands.

"We have no more information to share at this stage. The medical examiner will prepare a report in due course, but right now we need you to come and formally identify the body. Would you like to ride with us? We can arrange transport home afterward."

"No, I'll take my own car. Thank you, officers. Just tell me where I have to go."

"You can follow us."

The woman cop appeared to want to protest, but her partner was already on his way to the door.

Then Thomas remembered that Hannah's car was blocking him in. He strode over to the kitchen door and opened it. Hannah leapt backward with a yelp; she had been listening with an ear pressed against the wood.

"Hannah, I need you to move your car. I'm going out."

"Do you think you should be driving? Why don't you let me take you? I don't mind. I can bring you back here afterward and warm up some soup or something." She had refilled her whiskey glass with white wine from the fridge. There was no sign of any attempt to make the suggested tea.

"Do you think *you* should be driving? No. I'm perfectly capable of looking after myself. Just move the car, please." With a regretful look at the coffee paraphernalia laid out on the counter, Thomas stalked back to the entrance hall where he grabbed his keys and coat, and waited for Hannah to exit ahead of him. He left his phone behind. *If it's important, they'll leave a voicemail.*

\*\*\*\*

Detective Barry Fish stood in the doorway of Professor Harmon's office and surveyed the room. The Crime Scene Investigation team had removed the body to the Medical Examiner's office, and he couldn't expect any information about cause of death or forensic results for twenty-four hours, maybe longer if the M.E. was backed up with other cases. He didn't yet have a reason to believe a crime had been committed. However, the axiom of police work that the first twenty-four hours are critical in any investigation ran through his head, along with that other maxim: it's usually the husband.

He hadn't met the husband yet; a patrol car had been dispatched to break the news. Barry had arrived on the scene along with the CSI unit. The students who had discovered the body were still hanging around and he needed to interview them, as well as the dead woman's boss, and the department secretary. He started with Professor Hersch, an elderly academic with a pompous style of speaking, who had nothing useful to contribute but took a long time to say it. Then he moved on to the secretary.

Anne Summers was a thin woman of about fifty. Her hair was drawn back from her face in a neat ponytail and her mouth was pinched. She wore clothes ordered from a catalog, sensible rather than stylish. She was able to give a crisp rundown of the comings and goings along the corridor that led to Geraldine Harmon's office. Her own workspace was around a corner and not in a direct sight line, but she was confident that no one could pass by without her noticing.

"Professor Harmon arrived at nine o'clock," the secretary stated. "She stopped to chat for a minute, then went along to her office. She didn't come out again."

"Not even to get a cup of coffee?" Barry noticed the coffee maker and fixings on the file cabinet behind the secretary's desk. "Or to go to the bathroom?"

"Geraldine always brought her own coffee with her, and she could get to the restroom without coming back here—" She reddened, realizing her mistake.

"Ah, so there's another way to approach the professor's office?" Barry's voice was gentle; no need to alienate the woman.

"Well, I suppose so, if you go left out the door of her office, but there's nothing down there except the restrooms and a storage room…and a fire exit."

"Where does the fire exit lead?" he prompted.

"To an alley where the trash cans are. But you can't come in that way. The door only opens outward."

Barry nodded, remembering several cases in his long career where a strategically-placed wedge had kept an entry or escape route open for criminally-minded individuals. "And then?"

"The girl arrived about ten minutes before ten o'clock. Professor Harmon holds office hours at ten so I assumed she was here for that. She didn't say anything to me." The secretary sniffed. "I'm invisible to most students. The young man did at least smile. He came about five minutes later."

"And then?"

"Um, the boy phoned me about ten past. I can't think why he didn't just walk down here. They live on their phones, these students. Anyway, he said the professor wasn't answering when he knocked. I told him she was there and to just go on in. Next thing, the girl comes staggering down the corridor looking green. She told me Professor Harmon was dead and that she'd called the police." Anne Summers looked affronted that this important task had not been left to her. "I telephoned Professor Hersch—he's the department chair—then I waited here with the girl for the police."

"You didn't go to see for yourself?"

"No! I'm not a..." She sounded shocked. "When Professor Hersch arrived, *he* went to look. The police arrived just a minute or two later."

"And the other student..." Fish consulted his notes. "Marco Johansen? He stayed with the body until the police arrived?"

"Ye-es, I suppose so. He's still around if you want to talk to him. And Aubrey, the girl. They'll be in Lecture Hall C. It's where Professor Harmon teaches her noon class." For the first time, the secretary lost her composure, pressing her hand to her mouth, her eyes filling. Barry had seen it many times: in the aftermath of a tragedy, adrenaline, perhaps mixed with a sense of self-importance, carries a witness forward until some detail—the inappropriate use of the present tense, for example—derails them.

He murmured a few consolatory words and strolled down to the lecture room. There he found a dozen or so students talking about the news the Department Chair had shared in his typical circuitous manner: class was canceled for today, and they should continue their critical reading of the assigned text, perhaps forming study groups, because it was uncertain when the Intro to Literature class would meet again as their instructor was—hrumph—indisposed. Perhaps, well, permanently indisposed. After Professor Hersch left, Aubrey gave a dramatic interpretation of his message, complete with a graphic description of her reaction: "I almost hurled chunks!"

Marco said nothing. He was the first to notice the detective's arrival. Fish was standing inside the door, listening. Marco recognized him as a cop at once: the wary stance, evenly balanced with feet apart, hands clasped in front. The clothes too: a well-cut blazer left unbuttoned for quick access to the shoulder holster, chinos, and black sneakers. Although closer to sixty than forty, this man was fit. He could probably beat Marco in a foot race, and wrestle to the ground any student in the room, even the football players.

Fish cleared his throat. The students swiveled toward him.

"Aubrey Peters? Marco Johansen? Could I have a word, please?"

Aubrey slouched forward, conscious of her classmates' eyes on her. She stopped in front of Fish and looked up at him with a smirk.

"Do I need a lawyer?" There were a few hastily suppressed giggles; perhaps that was the reaction Aubrey wanted, because she didn't wait for Barry to respond. Marco followed her out, and the detective came behind them.

"Mr. Johansen? Marco? Perhaps I could talk to you

first. That will give Ms. Peters time to think about whether she wants to call her lawyer." Fish smiled as he spoke and kept any hint of sarcasm out of his voice.

When the men were seated in the vacant classroom that Barry had scoped out for the interview, the detective introduced himself, then took down Marco's contact details.

"So, I understand you found Professor Harmon's body. Tell me about it."

With a minimum of guiding questions from the cop, Marco went through the events of the morning. When he finished speaking, Fish looked through his notes.

"And you didn't move the body?"

"Only her head. Like I told you, I moved her head to the side to see if she was still breathing. I put my cheek next to her mouth and nose: nothing. I'd already checked for a pulse in her neck and her wrist. I knew she was dead. I didn't touch anything else."

Fish nodded.

"Did you notice anything? Something in the room that struck you? Any detail that seemed strange?"

Marco shook his head.

"I'd never been in the prof's office before. It all looked normal to me. Why? Didn't she die of a heart attack or something? Is her death suspicious?"

"We don't know what she died of. We have to treat all unexplained deaths as suspicious until we know otherwise."

That seemed reasonable to Marco but he'd bet that Aubrey would make some huge murder mystery out of it. In telling their classmates the story, she'd already reinvented her role to make herself the star. *She* was the one who insisted on breaking into the office, suspecting something was wrong. It was *she* who determined Professor Harmon was dead and who raised the alarm. Marco didn't think this cool detective would buy it, but even so he was glad he'd been interviewed first.

"Thanks. Can you show Ms. Peters in?"

Aubrey's interview took much longer but added nothing. After she broke off her narrative a second time to respond to an incoming text, Fish asked her to turn the phone off. Then her responses became sullen and monosyllabic.

"Thank you, Ms. Peters. I have your contact information and if we need anything else, we'll be in touch."

"Shouldn't you give me your card so *I* can call *you* if I remember something? That's what they do on the cop shows." She had recovered some of her vivacity.

Fish shrugged and smiled.

"Sorry, fresh out of cards. Just call the police department. They'll find me."

He went back to the dead woman's office. This time he put on paper shoe covers and latex gloves. He entered and shut the door behind him. He walked behind the desk and half-crouched so his eyes were on a level with a person sitting there. Scanning the room carefully from this angle, Barry recognized that something was missing. It took a second for him to put a name to it: a computer. A battered leather briefcase stood under the desk. He looked through it: papers and journals, but the sleeve that accommodated a laptop was empty. He pulled open desk drawers for a cursory search, then moved over to the cupboards under the bookshelves that lined one wall. No laptop, iPad, or even a cell phone. Of course the phone might have been in the pocket of her clothes and gone with her to the M.E.'s office.

He returned to the desk. Although cluttered, it showed some system of organization: a pile of student papers to the left, some manila folders with lecture notes to the right, a leather- bound day planner pushed to one corner. He opened it. There were few entries, confirming his suspicion that Professor Harmon, like most people, organized her life digitally. A framed photo on another corner of the desk showed a couple on a beach. Hawaii, he guessed. The professor and her husband? In the center of the desk, where the dead woman's head had rested, was the student essay she had been working on. A wet spot blurred the typed words. Fish leaned in closer, noticing faint scratches on the surface of the desk above the paper. Had Professor Harmon clawed the wood in a death spasm? Or was this evidence of a struggle with an aggressor, someone holding her face down? He took a close-up photo with his phone, in case CSI had missed the marks, and made a mental note to ask the M.E. about them.

After stripping off the booties and gloves, Barry walked back to Anne Summers' desk.

"Do you have Professor Harmon's cell phone number?"

"Of course." The secretary pulled up a screen on her computer. "Do you want her e-mail address as well?"

"Couldn't hurt," Fish replied, and wrote them both down. As he left the building to walk back to his car, he tapped in the professor's phone number. He had reached the police-issued Ford SUV by the time voicemail kicked in. He didn't leave a message, deciding to wait until cause of death was established to get the tech guys on it. They would be able to access phone records and the professor's dot-edu e-mail account. But the absence of a computer in her office nagged at him, as did the marks on the desk. They were not in parallel lines, as might be expected from clawing nails, but sketched a rough triangle. If made by the dying woman, what did they signify? What message was she trying to send in her last seconds?

Chapter 4

Cindy slept for a solid four hours. When she woke about lunchtime, her first thought was of Jesús. She'd been cleaning the bathrooms when he left with the crowd after breakfast, a mass of men dispersing into the still-dark streets. She wondered where he would go and whether he would return as a regular to the Mission. Would she see him again?

Her landscaping business was more or less shut down for the winter. She had a couple of clean-up jobs to do for regular customers, but she could handle those alone and on her own schedule when weather permitted. Otherwise, she spent her time fiddling around at home, cleaning and maintaining tools, or making calls to the contract laborers she used during the summer season to make sure they were hanging in there, hadn't been deported or anything. This afternoon she planned to make a start on the books to get ready for filing taxes, but after an hour of setting up the necessary spreadsheets, she got restless and decided to take Josie, her blue heeler mix, for a walk. Josie was a rescue dog, thirty pounds of muscle and unconditional love, not too pretty but fiercely loyal.

The rain had eased up, and a couple of patches of blue sky showed over the bay. Cindy invited Josie up into the passenger seat of the truck and drove down to the waterfront park. Quite a few dog walkers had the same idea, and she soon tired of restraining Josie, who saw all other animals as threats. Leaving the manicured park and cutting through an industrial area where long-haul trucks loaded up, she emerged on some wasteland. Here, a narrow creek made its way to the saltwater, and Josie could be allowed off-leash to explore brackish smells and roll in crud.

"You'll be riding in the back of the truck on the way home, my girl," Cindy told the dog. She often had one-sided conversations with Josie, but now the animal was too entranced with a dead fish to pay any attention. Cindy's thoughts returned to Jesús. She wondered why he fascinated her. Perhaps because he seemed out of place at the Mission with his tragic face and artist's hands. He might have stepped out of a Renaissance painting—Saint Sebastian awaiting martyrdom; an El Greco Christ on the way to Calvary. The cross he wore with the unusual symbol etched on it supported that impression. Perhaps he was a defrocked priest? A runaway monk?

Cindy shook her head to empty it of fantasies and called for Josie. It was five o'clock and getting dark. She'd stop for a beer on the way home, then pull something out of the freezer to microwave for supper on the sofa. She had a novel to finish reading.

She didn't see Marco at first when she entered the Bluebird Brewery with a vigorously toweled-down Josie at her heels. The Bluebird was her favorite watering hole not just for the quality of the beer but because it allowed dogs. The cavernous former school bus garage had retained much of its rough industrial vibe. Gleaming tanks and stacked kegs were corralled at one end of the garage behind a ten-foot-high chain-link fence.

Mismatched stools grouped around workbenches accommodated the patrons, of whom there were few on an early November evening. The only artwork on the walls consisted of radiator grills and headlights from the building's former use, and the familiar company logo over the bar.

Cindy picked up her hazy IPA, thanked the barman, and turned to review the room. She spotted Marco sitting alone in a dim corner. He raised his glass to her and she walked over, followed by Josie.

" 'Of all the gin joints in all the towns in all the world, she walks into mine.' " Cindy grinned at Marco. He was too young to get the *Casablanca* reference, but he smiled back anyway and indicated the stool next to his. Josie busied herself checking out Marco's jeans from knee to ankle.

"Nice dog," he said, extending a hand for Josie to sniff.

"Well, you'd think so…" Cindy said, all serious. Marco withdrew his hand hurriedly, then realized she was teasing. They chatted about the dog, the weather, the Bluebird, and how they both liked that it didn't pretend to be anything other than a place to hang out and drink good beer. From time to time they lapsed into companionable silence, and Cindy was pleased that the ease with which they got along at the Mission carried over to other settings.

After Marco yawned for the second time in as many minutes, Cindy peered at him.

"You didn't manage to catch up on sleep today, then?"

"No, I had class. Well, I was supposed to have class," Marco shook his head and blinked his eyes in any effort to regain alertness. "It's been a strange day, to be honest. My professor died. I found her body."

Cindy understood Marco's fatigue might be emotional as well as physical. As he told her the details of his day, she listened with the occasional nod or sympathetic comment. She held back from asking questions, knowing he needed to process this death in his own time.

"I didn't even really know her, but I liked her. She seemed…kind."

"Mmm. Can I get you another? What are you drinking?" Cindy gestured at his empty glass.

"Root beer. Just a schooner, please."

Cindy raised her eyebrows but said nothing. The Bluebird made its own root beer too, and it was supposed to be excellent. When she returned with the drinks, Marco was frowning.

"I keep thinking there was something off, something I should have noticed. I know it's weird, not rational."

Cindy remembered her own weird feeling about Jesús. She wondered whether to confide in Marco, but decided against it.

"Yeah, it must be unsettling. You're not working tonight? Want company? I've got a freezer full of pizza."

"Thanks, but I'll be okay. I've got a biology class to prep for." Marco gestured at Josie, who had arranged herself over his shoes and was fast asleep. "Look, I think she likes me, she really likes me!"

****

"I think I have to cancel the book club meeting."

Hannah stood in the doorway to Aubrey's bedroom and spoke to her daughter's back. Aubrey was lying curled up on her bed facing the wall. Hannah knew she wasn't asleep though; she could see the glow from her phone brighten and dim as Aubrey scrolled.

"You know, what with Gerry's... Tommy won't be up for it. That just leaves four of us, and I think Kwendi might be a tad put out to come for so few."

Her daughter grunted but did not change position.

"So do you think you could ask him to postpone until we're back up to strength?"

"What?" Aubrey turned her attention to her mother. "What are you talking about?"

"Kwendi Barbera! The author! Your kickboxing friend! Remember? You asked him to our next book club meeting?" Hannah ventured a step inside the bedroom, then froze at Aubrey's glare.

"I don't do that class anymore. I thought I told you." She reverted to her phone.

"Well, you didn't." Hannah was peeved but unsurprised at the glitch in communication with her daughter. "Do you have his number? I'll call him."

"No need. I never got around to talking to him. Why would I have his number, anyway?"

Hannah sighed and retreated to the living room. She considered sending an e-mail to the book club group, but thought perhaps she would call instead. If any of them hadn't heard about Geraldine's death, it would be harsh to read it in an e-mail, and a call would be an opportunity to chat, share what she knew and speculate about what she didn't.

She opened her contacts to find the numbers but was distracted by thoughts of Dave. Why hadn't he responded to her text? She'd told herself there were rules about phone use while driving, but he had to stop sometime to eat or pee. Maybe she should call him. If he didn't answer, she could leave a voicemail. But then she couldn't remember what time zone he might be in by now. She didn't want to irritate him by calling too late. And she didn't want to seem needy. Hannah despised those desperate women who latched onto every unattached male they met.

She really thought it was going to be different with Dave. The serendipity of their meeting, the ease with which they went from being strangers to being in bed together. And neither of them had been drunk! She'd call him tomorrow early.

"Hello? Maisie? It's Hannah, I'm afraid I have some sad news—"

"I heard! How awful. Do you know what she died of?"

By the time the call ended half an hour later, Hannah and Maisie Cornwall had analyzed, interpreted, and embroidered the few facts known about Geraldine Harmon's death, the reaction of the bereaved husband, and his future as an eligible widower, including financial status and culinary tastes. Hannah, as the mother of the person who found the body and Thomas Harmon's first visitor afterward, had the lion's share of the conversation, but Maisie's husband—who had been an eligible widower himself when she nabbed him—was a doctor. Although her husband was close to eighty and retired, Maisie had absorbed enough medical knowledge from him to be able to diagnose several possible causes of death.

Hannah left an ambiguous voicemail for Penny and Gus that was sure to elicit a call back. Only Diana LaTour was left to contact. Hannah checked the time, half-hoping it was too late to make the call. Diana had joined the group at Geraldine's invitation a couple of months ago. She looked about forty years old, but Hannah suspected plastic surgery and a rigorous exercise routine might disguise an earlier birthdate. Diana was unmarried, like Hannah, but childless and with more money. Diana intimidated her. Unconsciously sitting up straighter, Hannah tapped in the numbers.

"Hello?" Even Diana's voice sounded rich. "A great voice for radio," Hannah's ex would have said. "And a perfect body for TV," he would have added with a leer.

"Hi, it's Hannah Peters. I'm calling about book club. I expect you've heard."

"Heard what? That the author is gracing us with his presence?"

Oops. Because Gerry had introduced Diana as her old friend—"No, not old! My *good* friend!"—Hannah had assumed she would have been amongst those calls Tommy said he had to make. Now she would have to break the news. It was one thing to hash over the sudden death with Maisie, who matched Hannah in the gossip stakes, but another to summon the requisite empathy for a sensitive conversation with a woman she didn't much like.

"It's about Geraldine. Thomas didn't call you?"

"No." Diana sounded annoyed. "What about Geraldine?"

"I'm afraid I have sad news. Geraldine died this morning." Hannah bit her lip, searching for the bland phrases that accompanied such announcements in TV soap operas.

A long silence was followed by a strange gulping sound. Diana was crying! Hannah rushed to drown out the embarrassing sound of raw emotion.

"Yes. Very sudden. My daughter is one of her students. She found her in her office. Geraldine's office, not Aubrey's, I mean. Such a shock. Tommy is devastated, of course—"

"Is he?" Diana's sharp question interrupted Hannah's flow. What did she mean by that? Did Diana know something about Geraldine's marriage that she had hidden from Hannah? How could she find out what that was?

"You've known them for a long time, I suppose? Where did you meet?" She thought Diana wasn't going to answer, the pause went on so long. Then came a long, shuddering sigh as Diana pulled herself together.

"I met Geraldine at Oxford. We were students there." Her voice sounded weak. "Before she married…him. We always kept in touch, even though I lived overseas. Such a waste!" Diana broke down again, the awful choking noise making Hannah hold the phone away from her ear.

"Well, I'm so sorry for your loss—*our* loss. I really expected Thomas would have called you. But, um, I need to tell you that book club's been cancelled in view of… I'll e-mail you when we reschedule, and if I, er, hear anything else, you know, about *arrangements*."

Diana didn't respond. Hannah hurried through her goodbyes, glad to finish the call. Diana's reaction, together with the fact that Thomas had not called her about Geraldine's death, gave Hannah food for thought. Clearly there was no love lost between Diana and Thomas. Did Diana and Geraldine have an affair while students at Oxford? Had the affair been rekindled when Diana moved to town earlier in the year? Did Tommy find out, and—no, he wouldn't have! Although he did

40

act a little strange when she was at his house that morning. She'd put down his coldness to the result of shock, but maybe...? Alternatively, Geraldine, torn between two lovers and wracked with guilt, killed herself. That seemed unlike her—she always seemed so grounded and cheerful.

Hannah glanced at her watch. It really was too late now to call Maisie back and talk this through. Maybe Aubrey was still awake.

****

Diana took a deep drag on her cigarette and exhaled a plume of smoke into the night. She rarely smoked, and never inside, but the news had knocked her sideways. She needed *something*, and having consumed her daily allowance of calories, comfort eating—or comfort drinking, for that matter—was out of the question. She kept a little metal box with a lighter and a pack of Gauloises tucked away in a planter on the patio for such occasions.

Geraldine, dead? She couldn't grasp the fact. It must be a mistake, or some kind of bizarre trick that awful woman Hannah was playing. Then the words hit her again like a tsunami: Geraldine, dead. She started shaking and had to sit down in one of the Adirondack chairs. The wood was damp and hard. She was reminded of that winter in Oxford when she first met Geraldine, the uncomfortable benches in the lecture halls, the cold that seeped from ancient stone walls.

****

Diana was friendless and out of place. Oxford was her grandfather's idea, not hers, but with no siblings or parents who might support her resistance, she had acquiesced. Lingering outside Blackwell's bookstore at the beginning of her second term, she heard an American accent. She turned to see a group of students in lively conversation, a short, auburn-haired girl with the familiar accent at its center. The group dispersed and the American girl entered the bookstore. Diana followed her with no particular intention other than to be close to a voice from home.

"Are you stalking me?" The girl's warm smile took any sting out of the accusation. Diana had trailed her from New Fiction on the ground floor, through Biography and up to Literary Criticism on the floor above.

"No! I mean, I overheard you talking and I wondered where you came from. In the States, that is," Diana stammered, her face reddening.

"Boston. I'm post-grad at Oriel," the girl responded, sticking out a hand. "Geraldine Riley. And you?"

"Diana LaTour. I'm from California. First year at St. Hilda's." Diana named one of the women's colleges located on the edge of town.

"Ooh, poor you! Why don't you come back to my rooms for tea before you make the long trek to the suburbs? They don't have the book I wanted here anyway."

Geraldine's friendship turned Diana's life around. In later years, Diana would say she saved it. Through Geraldine, she was invited to parties, met interesting fellow students, and became involved in university clubs. By the time Geraldine completed her master's degree in English Literature and returned to America, Diana had established a wide social circle and evolved into a confident young woman. When she in turn completed her studies, she decided to remain in the UK, found a job in London with a marketing firm, and eventually started her own business developing consumer research tools.

People assumed Diana sold her successful company after she received the cancer diagnosis, but negotiations were already at an advanced stage before she consulted a doctor about her symptoms. Growing the business had devoured her life for long enough. She intended to cash in and kick back while she was young enough to enjoy it. She planned extended trips, including back to the States. Work had prevented her attending Geraldine's wedding, and she promised her friend she'd make up for it by spending a few weeks with her during the summer.

Instead, Geraldine came to London to look after Diana post-surgery and through the nightmare of chemotherapy. For the first two months of a sabbatical year, Geraldine cooked and cleaned, drove Diana to her appointments, read Jane Austen aloud to her, and held her hand through crying jags that seemed to last hours. She was willing to stay longer, but then Thomas arrived. He claimed he'd come to do research in England for a novel he was writing, and that he wouldn't "get in the way." However, his broad hints about the projects Geraldine had lined up for her year without classes to teach, and references to their busy social life at home made Diana feel guilty. His presence spoiled the easy camaraderie from their Oxford days that had reestablished itself between the women. At Diana's insistence that she would be fine, a reluctant Geraldine departed for home, Thomas at her elbow wearing a smug smile.

Following a rigorous holistic regimen, Diana recovered her health. She indulged her taste for travel, and developed an interest in opera. She bought a dilapidated farmhouse in Norfolk and painstakingly restored it, only to discover she didn't enjoy country life, so she sold it and returned to London. She spent lavishly on her wardrobe and grooming. Never a beauty, Diana matured into a sinewy elegance.

The women maintained a frequent correspondence, and Facetimed when they could work out the time difference between London and the West Coast. Geraldine's e-mails were full of wry humor: anecdotes about her students and other faculty members, little digs about Diana's Anglomania. Then in June, the fourth anniversary of Diana's diagnosis, she noticed a change in tone. A note of panic crept into Geraldine's closings: *when are you coming to visit? I* have *to see you.* When Diana probed during video calls, Geraldine laughed it off. Diana suspected Thomas was lurking somewhere out of camera range.

On impulse, Diana took a short-term lease on a furnished house near Geraldine's college, and booked a flight. She found her friend strangely diminished; the ebullient student she had known in Oxford and the empathetic friend in London had disappeared and been replaced by an anxious middle-aged woman. The person Diana remembered would never have put up with a lightweight phony like Hannah, one of Geraldine's book club members. There was something out of kilter in her relationship with Thomas, too. Diana hadn't warmed to Geraldine's husband, but she was wary of letting jealousy color her perceptions. After a few weeks' observation, she was convinced Geraldine was tiptoeing around Thomas, smoothing over any potential disagreement and accommodating his rather rigid routines.

Geraldine came over for drinks—on her own—three weeks after the fall semester started. Diana came straight to the point.

"You seem worried about something. What is it?"

Geraldine walked around the room, picking up objects and putting them down, scanning the titles on the bookcase, avoiding Diana's eye.

"The guy that owns this place is a colleague. Well, he's in the history department, but we sit on some faculty committees together."

"Come on, Gerry. Stop stalling. What's wrong?"

Geraldine gave a brittle laugh.

"You haven't called me Gerry since Oxford. Thomas hates that name. The only other person who calls me Gerry is Hannah, and she's—" Geraldine broke off. She took a seat on the sofa and sipped her wine. Diana waited.

"It's probably just menopause. I keep imagining I'm being spied on. I know, it sounds ridiculous, but…" Geraldine looked into her glass, still unable to meet Diana's sympathetic gaze. "There's other stuff too."

"Like what?" Diana asked.

"I keep losing things. No, not losing them. Someone's moving them." Again, the false laugh. "It's crazy, isn't it? It must be menopause. Or early onset Alzheimer's." She looked at Diana then. *This is what she's scared of: Alzheimer's,* Diana thought.

"Have you seen a doctor?"

Geraldine shook her head.

"Well, make an appointment. I'll go with you. Don't tell Thomas." Diana didn't quite know why she added that warning, but it seemed essential.

\*\*\*\*

Diana lit a second cigarette, breaking her own rules. Geraldine would not keep that doctor's appointment now. She would never know if her sense that someone was watching her and moving things around was based in reality or was the product of hormonal imbalance or brain disease. Did it matter? Not to Geraldine now, but it did to her friend.

Diana was not going to let the matter rest.

Chapter 5

By the time Dave had completed the trip paperwork and driven his own car back to the St. Louis suburb where he and Joanne lived with their two kids, the time was one a.m. He crept into the bedroom, took his clothes off, and slid under the covers next to his wife. She stirred.

"Cold feet," she murmured, but did not draw away from him as he curled his body around hers. She fell asleep again in seconds, and seconds later he was dead to the world too.

When he woke it was past nine o'clock and the house was quiet. He had slept through the noisy chaos of getting the children ready for school and out the door. Luxuriating in the knowledge that he had forty-eight hours at home before he was due out on the road again, he showered and dressed in sweats. Joanne was busy at the sink when he came downstairs. He poured himself a cup from the coffeemaker and perched on one of the stools at the breakfast bar. Something was missing: the smell of bacon frying. His usual welcome home breakfast was bacon and eggs with a side of cheese grits. Maybe they were out of eggs. He'd do the grocery shopping later to give Joanne a break.

"Hey, sorry for not helping with the kids. I was bushed!"

Joanne's back was still toward him; she stood motionless, her hands hanging at her sides.

"Who's this woman that keeps texting and e-mailing you—this Hannah?" she said through a clenched jaw.

"What?" Dave's body stiffened as his brain raced. *How does Joanne know about Hannah?* Then he noticed his phone face down on the bar. He'd left it there when he came in last night, along with his car keys.

"Who is she?" Joanne turned, and he saw she'd been crying.

"Aw, honey, she's no one. Just an old lady. I helped change her tire. The spare looked kinda sketchy so I followed her to make sure she got home okay. I don't know how she got my number. She was grateful, I guess, so maybe she called the company and they gave it to her." Dave was aware he was talking too much, making things up on the fly. He reached out a hand, but Joanne batted it away.

"Old lady?"

Dave jumped on her question.

"Yeah! She was sixty at least. She told me she had a grown-up daughter."

"Liar!" She pulled her own phone out of her jeans back pocket and slapped it down in front of him. He was scared to look, but she pointed at the screen, forcing him to follow her finger. "Sixty, my ass!"

Hannah's image, photoshopped and airbrushed, smiled seductively up from her Facebook profile page. Dave searched for an excuse.

"She doesn't look like that. Maybe you got the wrong Hannah. There must be dozens on Facebook." He could see she wasn't buying it. He changed track. "Joanne, honey, she means nothing to me—to us! Just a woman I helped out with a flat tire. She invited me to dinner to show her appreciation, that's all."

"And you gave her your number."

"Only so's she could text directions to her house, y'know, for dinner."

"If you followed her home, you already knew where she lived." Joanne had adopted an acridly sweet tone, but Dave knew she'd become shrill if he said the wrong thing. His wife was twice as smart as he was, and super-talented with anything on the internet. He had no doubt she'd found Hannah on social media in twenty seconds flat.

"Yeah, you're right. I don't know why I gave her my number. I was just stupid, didn't realize she'd start cyber-stalking me." He put on his best hang-dog look. "I'm real sorry." He wondered if he should risk reaching out to give her a hug, then decided against it.

Joanne fixed him with a cold stare. She nodded, picked up her phone and glanced at it before replacing it in her pocket. She turned back to the sink.

"Well, I think she'll be real sorry too, when all her four hundred and forty-four Facebook friends find out what a filthy slut she is. Oh, I should say four hundred and forty-five. She just accepted my friend request."

\*\*\*\*

Barry Fish waited until two days after Geraldine Harmon's body was found to call the Medical Examiner's office. Some assistant gave him the "don't call us, we'll call you" run-around. Nevertheless, he persisted until he was put through to Tariq Ali Khan.

"So, Doc, Geraldine Harmon. Whatcha got for me?"

"I completed the autopsy on Professor Harmon yesterday, but we are still awaiting test results on blood, stomach contents, and other residues." Tariq's clipped Pakistani accent and correct manner of speaking made him sound like he was reading from a written report. Barry liked Tariq—he was reliable and thorough, but the M.E.'s formality brought out the slang of *film noir* in the detective's communication style.

"C'mon, just the preliminaries. I'm treading water till you give me a cause of death. Natural causes or murder?" He pronounced it *moiduh* and got a chuckle out of Tariq.

"I really don't know until I get the laboratory results. What I *can* tell you is that the time of death was between 8:30 a.m. and 9:30 a.m. on Wednesday morning. The deceased was a well-nourished female, forty-nine years old, with no obvious signs of disease or injury that might have caused her death."

"Anything else?" Fish urged.

"There was slight bruising at the sides of the neck."

"Strangled?"

"No, cause of death was not strangulation. The airway was not damaged. The bruising was *ante mortem* by at least an hour."

"So the killer held the dame down while he injected a slow-acting poison!" Fish was enjoying himself. Tariq laughed again.

"What a lurid imagination you have, Detective. No, the bruising appears to have been caused by someone standing in front of the professor and gripping her around the neck with two hands, thumbs toward the assailant. As I stated, the bruising is superficial."

*And an hour before she died*, Barry thought. *Breakfast time.* "Hmm. Did you find a phone in her personal belongings?"

"No. When Professor Harmon's husband came to formally identify the body, he posed the same question.

He was most keen to reclaim it and her other personal effects."

Barry ended the call, extracting a promise from the M.E. that he would hurry the lab to finish their tests. He checked with the duty sergeant for the whereabouts of the patrol officers who made the initial visit to inform Thomas Harmon of his wife's death. As luck would have it, Officer Melinda Dinero was at the precinct, and he tracked her down to the breakroom where she was fighting with the candy machine.

"Here, let me help." Fish's well-placed slam dislodged the hovering chocolate bar and it fell into the drawer at the base of the machine. "Did you file a report yet on your death notice call the other day?"

"Yeah, but there wasn't much to say. Thomas Harmon already knew about his wife, and he drove himself to the morgue." Melinda's ambition was to be promoted to detective, and she was glad that she, not her partner, was on hand for Barry Fish.

"Your impressions of the husband?"

Melinda smiled. This might be her big chance. She thought for a moment before speaking.

"He seems like a cold fish." Melinda flashed on the detective's last name and mentally kicked herself. "Of course, everyone reacts to shock differently, but he was more irritated than anything. That might have been because of this awful woman who'd rushed over to be first to break the news. Then, at the morgue, he made the ID and left. Oh, he did ask to take his wife's personal stuff with him, which I thought was a bit strange. The M.E. explained everything had to be examined and we'd let him know when he could collect them. That's all."

"Thanks, that's helpful," Fish said. "How would you

like to give me a ride out to his house now? I need to speak to him, and I'd like you there too." He thought Melinda seemed on the ball for being so young and new to the Department.

"Yes, sir! I'll just go clear it with the desk sergeant."

"Okay, but it's Barry—or Fish, if you like. Not 'sir.'"

In the patrol car on the way over to the Harmon house, Melinda held the wheel in a death grip and drove well within the speed limit, anxious not to ruin this opportunity with a fender bender. Fish asked a few questions about her background and her experience with the Department so far, trying to put her at her ease. They parked, and Fish held up a hand to stop her exiting the vehicle while he surveyed the neighboring residences. When he was satisfied, he motioned for her to get out.

"Take notes, will you? And observe."

Melinda nodded, unsure exactly what she was supposed to observe. They approached the front door. Fish rang the doorbell. After a few seconds, the door cracked open about six inches and Thomas Harmon's face appeared in the gap. Fish introduced himself and held out his badge for inspection.

"And of course you've already met Officer Deniro. We have a few more questions. May we come in?"

Harmon said nothing but stepped back so they could enter. He followed them into the living room and indicated that they should sit on the sofa. He remained standing.

"Well, do you have any news? Are you going to release my wife's body? I have to make arrangements, you know." The word Melinda had used—irritated—still characterized his demeanor.

"I'm afraid the Medical Examiner has not yet completed his report." The detective continued before Harmon could complain. "The morning of your wife's death, I believe you told Officer Deniro that you had breakfast with your wife. What time was that?"

"I don't see—I suppose about eight a.m." Harmon sat down, making a show of exasperation by rolling his eyes and sighing.

"Can you be more specific? Was she already up and dressed before you came downstairs?"

"Yes, it was a perfectly normal morning. Geraldine's alarm went off at 7:30, she got up, got dressed, and came down to the kitchen to put the kettle on. When I heard the kettle whistle, I put my dressing gown on and joined her for breakfast."

"What did you each have for breakfast?"

"Honestly, Detective, I cannot see the relevance of what we ate!"

Fish waited, an apologetic smile playing on his lips.

"I had toast with honey. She had cereal and fruit—blueberries, I believe. We each drank a cup of Earl Grey tea." Harmon spoke with sarcastic precision. "She left for the university as usual at 8:15."

"And what did you speak about over breakfast?"

Harmon staged a little explosion, throwing his hands in the air and rising from his chair.

"How on earth can I be expected to remember what we talked about? This is utterly ridiculous!"

Barry and Melinda remained seated, Melinda scribbling in her notebook, Barry looking bored.

"Did you have an argument?" Barry kept his voice flat.

"What?"

"Did you put your hands around her throat?" Now there was an edge to Barry's tone.

Harmon's mouth dropped open. It took a moment before he collected himself enough to respond.

"I've told you I don't remember what we talked about."

Fish looked at Melinda and nodded, as if to confirm a previous understanding, then turned back to Harmon.

"Forensic science has made terrific advances. They can now lift fingerprints off the surface of human skin. As well as DNA, of course."

"I'm asking you to leave. I have no more to say to you without my attorney present." Harmon gathered up the shreds of his dignity and marched to the front door. Melinda, a little shocked at Barry's tactics, put her notebook away and followed, trailed by the detective.

Once outside, and with the door shut behind them, Barry exhaled a long breath.

"Now let's see what happens."

Instead of driving back to the precinct, they hovered by the police car for a few minutes. A door opened two houses down from the Harmons' and an elderly woman came out to stand on the front step.

"Bingo!" said Barry. "There's always someone who takes it on themselves to be Neighborhood Watch. Come on."

He gave a wave to the woman and set off in her direction. Melinda finally understood why they had used the patrol car instead of the detective's unmarked vehicle, and why they had been so slow to leave the scene.

**\*\*\*\***

Diana rose at four a.m., checked the European stock

indexes on her laptop, and called her broker in London with instructions. The quiet of the early morning hours pleased her. Plus, half the business day still lay ahead in Europe. When she sold her company, she had invested the proceeds in shares. Although she consulted financial advisors, she liked to keep a close eye on her investments. It paid off. Her wealth had doubled in five years.

Then she brewed coffee, poured herself a cup—black, no sugar—and opened her inbox. With a few keystrokes she assembled all the emails Geraldine had sent her since the start of the year. She wanted to go through them to find a clue to what had been bothering her friend. Maybe there was a pattern Diana had overlooked when she had read them one by one days or weeks apart.

During Spring Break in late March, Geraldine had attended—without Thomas—an academic conference in Santa Fe, New Mexico. The title of the conference was "Literature and Social Change," and Geraldine had presented a paper on Dickens as a social reformer. *Deathly boring: most of the audience was asleep after ten minutes!* she wrote with her usual self-deprecating humor. But there was something, or someone, at the conference that grabbed her interest: a young journalist had written a novel set in Central America that she described in the email as *refreshing, urgently real but somehow allegorical as well*. He was not one of the presenters but had approached Geraldine privately and subsequently emailed her the manuscript to read. Diana remembered teasing her about it on a subsequent FaceTime session.

"So, how good-looking was this young journalist?"

Diana asked. Geraldine was in her office at the university, so Thomas wouldn't be wandering past to eavesdrop on their conversation.

"Oh, stop it. It isn't like that at all. I really like the novel, and I feel sorry for him. He's taking a big risk because the story exposes real-life political corruption. If he published the information in a newspaper in his home country he'd be arrested, maybe worse, so he has to disguise it as fiction."

"And you're going to help him, aren't you?" Diana loved her friend, but sometimes her bleeding heart was exasperating.

Geraldine looked downcast. "I'm not sure I can. I tried to get the department here to give him a Writer in Residence position, but Hersch says there's no budget. And now I can't even reach Michael—that's the journalist's name. The number he gave me is out of service, and I don't have any other contact information. I spoke to the organizers of the conference, but they say he was a late, in-person registrant, and they don't know how to reach him either."

"Well, if you have his manuscript, I'm sure he'll turn up," Diana tried to reassure her.

Geraldine did not mention the missing journalist or his manuscript in later emails, at least not directly. In May, with end-of-semester exams looming, Geraldine seemed overwhelmed with work. Her emails were short, and she wasn't available for video chats.

On May 20, she wrote: *I think I've made a big mistake. You always told me to be more careful with my possessions, not lend them to just anyone. And this wasn't even mine! I always thought the written word was like air or water: everyone should have access. But*

*words are weapons too, and can be turned against you
even by people you trust.*

Diana replied, asking what this ambiguous message
meant, but obtained no clarification. Reviewing it now,
it occurred to her that Geraldine must have given the
manuscript to someone, a colleague or perhaps
Thomas—he was a writer too—and they had revealed its
veiled content to the people Michael (last name
unknown) feared.

The three emails received from Geraldine after May
20 contained the pleas that had provoked Diana's
transatlantic move: *When are you coming to visit? I have
to see you.*

****

Diana had never owned a car, although she had
learned to drive as a teenager. In London, she took the
ubiquitous black taxicabs. If she went to the country for
the weekend, she hired a car, usually something flashy
and fun. When she arrived in the States and realized she
needed a consistent mode of transportation, she signed a
six-month lease on a bland Korean-made sedan.

She was glad now of the vehicle's ordinariness, as
she sat parked a few doors down from Geraldine's—now
Thomas's—home. She was not quite ready to confront
the man, although she was convinced that he had
somehow played a part in the circumstances leading to
her friend's death. She wanted to observe and follow
him. Perhaps her surveillance would unnerve him and
force him into revealing something.

She watched the police car draw up, and the
occupants' leisurely approach to Thomas's front door.
The officers stayed inside for less than ten minutes but
were in no hurry to depart the scene after they emerged.

They called on a neighbor's house and stayed for a while.

When the patrol car finally pulled away from the curb, Diana debated with herself whether she should maintain her stakeout or follow the police back to the police department and share her vague suspicions with the investigators. She decided to follow: they might in turn give her some information.

****

Barry Fish asked Melinda to walk back to his cubicle with him. The young patrol officer had good observation skills, and he intended to get her reassigned to the detective squad—which currently consisted of only him—if this case turned out to have legs. Signaling to Melinda to take his chair, he hitched one haunch onto the desk and dialed Tariq's number. He wanted to see if the M.E.'s report had been completed. This time he was put straight through.

"Yes, I know. You should have had the report by now." The doctor sounded harried. "The laboratory results are unclear…confusing. I have asked for additional tests, and I am going to examine the body again."

Fish resisted his usual banter and waited for elucidation.

"There is evidence of a sedative in the stomach contents. Not much had entered the bloodstream so it was recently ingested, perhaps with her breakfast, possibly dissolved in her morning coffee."

"She always brought her coffee with her to the office," Barry interrupted. "But there was no coffee cup on her desk when the body was found."

"Hmm. In any case, the amount absorbed would only have rendered her sleepy," the doctor said. "The reason why the results took so long was not the stomach content analysis, but the presence of an unfamiliar chemical in the bloodstream."

"She was poisoned?" Fish switched his phone to speaker, and placed it on the desk between him and Melinda. "I've put you on speaker so my colleague, Officer Dinero, can hear."

Melinda suppressed a grin at the word "colleague" and pulled out her notebook and pencil.

"Well, not exactly. The chemical in question comes from a plant that grows in South America. It was used for medicinal and ritual purposes by native populations for centuries, but with deforestation, the plant has become very rare. There is almost no scientific literature on its properties." Tariq paused. "I cannot say it caused or contributed to her death without further research."

"You said you were going to look at the body again. Why?" asked Barry.

"To see if there's an injection site. If this chemical was injected, a very small needle must have been used, because I already inspected her skin." Some of the M.E.'s confidence seemed to have left him. "I will let you know as soon as I have more information, but other than saying Professor Harmon's heart stopped beating, I cannot give you a cause of death."

After ending the call, Barry turned to Melinda.

"An unexplained death has become a suspicious death. Maybe we have probable cause for a search warrant at the Harmon residence. What do you think?"

Melinda, who was more familiar with traffic tickets than search warrants, nodded uncertainly. "But what about the parked car that the neighbor spotted? Shouldn't we follow that up?"

"There's always a nosy neighbor with a theory. She didn't get the license plate number or even the make. It's too vague." Barry noticed Melinda's frown. "But, yes, we'll follow it up if we get nothing on the husband."

Melinda suspected that the detective dismissed the tip because the neighbor was an elderly woman. She didn't voice the thought, and was saved from further discussion by the arrival of the duty sergeant. He walked up with a piece of paper in his hand.

"There's a lady out front wants to speak to you. Name of…" He consulted the paper. "Diana Latour. Says she's a friend of Geraldine Harmon."

"What's she like?"

"Kinda hoity-toity accent. Forties—too old for you," he joked.

"Okay, put her in the interview room. Want to tag along?" This last to Melinda, who was only too glad to accompany the detective. "Bring your notebook."

When he entered the interview room, he understood why the sergeant had called her a lady. Diana Latour was slim, posture-perfect, and her understated clothes—narrow black pants, crisp white shirt, and herringbone tweed jacket—whispered expense. She wore minimal makeup skillfully applied, and her straight dark hair was precisely cut in clean angles that echoed her jawline.

"Please, take a seat." Barry indicated the chairs, two on each side of a metal table bolted to the floor. The room was windowless and bare except for a large mirror on one wall allowing witnesses in an adjacent space to view the occupants. Diana glanced at the mirror. Barry smiled as he sat down opposite her.

"Sorry about the accommodations, but don't worry; there's no one next door and the recording equipment's off. Melinda will just make a few notes, if that's okay."

Diana nodded.

"So how long had you known Professor Harmon?" Barry eased into the interview, restraining for the moment his curiosity about what had brought this elegant woman to the police station.

"Twenty-five years, but until August I lived in London, so we didn't see much of each other. We corresponded and talked on video links." Diana leaned forward. She saw no need for these preliminaries. "I have concerns about Geraldine's death. I'd noticed she was not her usual self, and two weeks ago I asked her what was going on. She told me some disturbing things."

She paused to think through what she wanted to say. Barry waited.

"Do you know what I mean by 'gaslighting'?"

"I think so," Barry responded. "It's when someone tries to persuade another person that what they understand to be real is not; to make them doubt reality."

"Exactly." Diana took a deep breath before continuing. "Geraldine said she'd noticed things were going missing, or they'd turn up some place different from where she'd left them. She was worried she was losing her mind, that she had Alzheimer's, but I did some research and she had none of the symptoms described. She was as sharp as ever."

"Did she see a doctor?" Barry wondered if early-stage Alzheimer's would show up in an autopsy. Dr. Ali hadn't mentioned anything like that.

"I suggested she make an appointment. I was going to go with her. But she died before… There's something else; it might be irrelevant."

"Go on," Barry urged, glancing sideways to make

sure Melinda was noting it all down.

"In May, she emailed me that she'd lost something important, something that belonged to someone else. I think it was the manuscript of a novel she'd been entrusted with at a conference in March."

"But she didn't tell you what she'd lost?"

"No. As I said, it might be unconnected." Diana looked away, wondering if it all sounded too thin, perhaps hysterical. "Can you tell me how she died? I didn't see anything in the news, and the university is just saying 'sudden and unexpected.' "

"What did her husband tell you?"

Diana stiffened. She had determined not to mention her suspicions of Thomas—that *would* sound hysterical.

"Nothing. We haven't spoken."

*Interesting*, thought Fish. *Such a close friend of the wife, but not in touch with the husband.*

"The autopsy report hasn't been issued yet. All I can do is confirm that the death was sudden." An idea occurred to him. "Do you think Professor Harmon was worried enough about her mental health to consider suicide?"

"No!" Diana's reply was immediate. "She made the doctor's appointment, and was carrying on with her life. She loved her job; she wouldn't—"

Barry could see she was shaken. Behind Diana's poise and self-assurance was a woman with deep feelings for her friend. She could be an ally in the search for a motive if it turned out there was foul play. He shouldn't have raised the possibility of suicide; there was no evidence to support it. That was the problem: there was little evidence to support any explanation for Geraldine Harmon's death.

With the exchange of contact details, and promises to be in touch if anything new came up, the interview terminated.

Chapter 6

Thomas had met Geraldine at the launch of a novel at one of Boston's many independent bookstores. He was living in the city after a few years chronicling town council meetings and high school football games as a reporter on a small New Hampshire paper. Now he held a position with a monthly magazine modeled on *Better Homes and Gardens*. Although the publication failed to offer Thomas the chance to write the "think pieces" he knew he was capable of, it did mean he had time to pursue his own goal of writing the Great American Novel.

Geraldine stood on the lowest rungs of an academic career, having completed her PhD but a long way from tenure. Although she was several years younger than he, Thomas was impressed by the authority with which she expressed her opinions, when they went for coffee after the event.

"He shouldn't attempt to write from a woman's POV," she told him, referring to the author whose next best seller they had just previewed. "He fails completely to understand the female psyche."

"Hmm," was Thomas's only response. He'd been playing with a female protagonist for a series of short stories that might just evolve into a novel. He wasn't ready to discuss his work with this new acquaintance, but he thought he should make note of her speech patterns and gestures for future use. Not her clothes, though. At that time in her life, Geraldine had no money or taste for fashion. She shopped at thrift stores with an eye to warmth and washability.

Thomas's girlfriends in the past usually lasted about six months before one party or the other lost interest. The relationships faded without acrimony; he was still friends with a couple of them. Once, in college, he had even fancied himself in love—with a professor's wife, his Emma Bovary, the risk of discovery adding spice to the sex—but even then he experienced a kind of detachment, as if he were observing the affair rather than participating in it. Now, in his middle-thirties, he felt a need for something more permanent. Would Geraldine be The One?

They started dating. The sex was good, but the conversations even better. Thomas loved discussing literature with Geraldine; she was knowledgeable and funny. Her enjoyment of life was contagious; Thomas found himself questioning the habitual cynicism he used as a shield against emotion. They passed the six-month frontier effortlessly. However, he hesitated to say the L word or suggest they move in together. He had never shared his living space even in college. As for marriage? The specter of his parents' failed relationship made him wary.

Then Geraldine was offered a tenure-track assistant professorship at a liberal arts college in Washington State. On New Year's Eve, shortly after the one-year anniversary of their first meeting, Thomas took Geraldine for drinks at an elegant downtown hotel. The place was lavishly decorated for the holidays. Guests, dressed for the evening's festivities, passed through the lobby bar, talking and laughing in loud, inebriated voices.

Geraldine was excited about her new job. "It's a beautiful campus, surrounded by pine forests and mountains. You know, except for my Masters at Oxford, I've lived in Boston all my life. It's time for me to move."

"What does your family think about it?" Thomas asked. Geraldine was the youngest child in a sprawling Irish Catholic family. Her brothers and sisters had all married and stayed within a few miles of home. Thomas hoped that her parents were pressuring her to turn down a job that would take her across the country. He wanted things to stay as they were while he became comfortable with the idea of a long-term relationship. He almost resented Geraldine for putting him on the spot, forcing him to declare himself before he was ready.

"They're almost as thrilled as I am," Geraldine continued. "Now that Dad's retired, he's talking about buying an RV and taking to the road!"

Thomas fidgeted with the little leatherette box in his pocket. He had purchased the ring at an antique store, opals in a Victorian gold setting, *not* a diamond, *not* an engagement ring.

"Let's get out of here. It's too noisy and crowded." He settled the check, and they donned coats, gloves and scarfs before stepping out into the cold.

Halfway across Boston Common, Thomas pulled Geraldine up the steps to the bandstand. They stood for a moment looking at the snow sparkling in the city lights.

"Geraldine, you've become so important to me. I want...I want...you to marry me." The instant he said the words, he panicked. *Was* that what he wanted? He fumbled in his pocket for the ring, while Geraldine stood, mouth open, speechless. "Look, I bought you this ring. It doesn't have to be an engagement ring. Just, don't go to the West Coast. Stay here with me." He realized he sounded pathetic, so he stopped speaking and waited for her to say something.

Geraldine closed her mouth, swallowed and spoke hesitantly. "I didn't expect... You never said anything..." She turned away, pursing her lips as if to suppress a smile. "Thomas, I'm very flattered, and I like you a lot, but I don't want to get married—to anyone. I'm not ready! This job is a fantastic opportunity, and I need to focus on that."

Thomas experienced a mixture of emotions: he had not anticipated that she would turn him down, and he felt affronted. That she would put a low-ranking position at some unimportant college ahead of him was inexplicable, and he kicked himself for showing he cared. But behind the outrage lurked a sense of relief. He concealed these contradictory feelings, as always, behind a cool façade. "Well, can I write to you, at least?"

Geraldine laughed. "Of course you can! I'll look forward to your letters. Writing is what you do best."

And he had written to her. Every two or three weeks, he related funny anecdotes from his Boston life, reviews of films he'd seen and books he'd read, and asked appropriate, non-invasive questions about her new life, professional and social. He labored over these letters to strike exactly the right tone: interested, but not desperate; witty but not arrogant. He challenged himself to seduce her with his writing, with "what he did best." Assisted by the fact that Geraldine was lonely so far from family and lifelong friends, and unprepared for the ruthless competition between faculty members of the English Department, the letters worked. When she returned for her summer break, Thomas renewed his proposal, she accepted, and started the new academic year as a married woman.

****

Thomas sat at his computer in the spare bedroom now converted into his study. He stared unfocused at the screen. The police visit had shaken him. How did they know about his fight with Geraldine on the morning of her death? He had been on the point of telling them that fighting with Geraldine was a routine occurrence, when he realized how that would sound. He'd managed to get rid of them, but what now? *It's always the husband.* He'd gathered that much from his viewing of TV crime dramas.

The doorbell rang. *Christ, they've come back!* His first thought was not to answer the door. That would solve nothing. He should at least see who it was. He crept downstairs and looked through the peephole in the front door. An elderly woman stood on the porch; she was carrying something wrapped in aluminum foil. Thomas recognized her as Ellie Somebody from two houses down the street. He may have spoken to her five times in the decade he and Geraldine had lived here. Her last name escaped him; Geraldine always took care of neighborhood relations. He opened the door.

"Oh, Thomas. I'm so very sorry for your loss. Geraldine was a lovely person." She thrust the foil-covered offering at him, leaving him no alternative but to take it. He looked around for somewhere to put it down but was afraid it might leave a ring on the handsome console table. Seeing his indecision, Ellie took the item back. "This needs to go in the fridge," she said over her shoulder as she marched toward the kitchen. *First Hannah, now this old biddy. Why can't they leave me alone?* Exasperated, he followed her.

"Macaroni and cheese, my special recipe with three different cheeses." She stowed the dish in the refrigerator and turned a sympathetic gaze back to Thomas. "I thought I should stop by to offer my condolences, and to let you know I've spoken to the police."

Thomas's heart gave a lurch. "What?" It was the first word he'd spoken to her.

"Yes, I saw them after they came away from your place and took the opportunity. I already mentioned it to Geraldine as she was getting into her car on Wednesday, the morning she, um… Well, she wouldn't have had the chance to tell you about it, I suppose." She paused to glance around the pristine kitchen, countertops clear, sink empty. "I guess you're expecting family to arrive. I shouldn't take up your time."

Thomas was beginning to understand how he should play this: newly bereaved, confused by grief. "No, no one's coming. I just haven't been able to do anything since…" He hung his head and waited for her to explain what she had said to Geraldine and the police. He was certain she would need no prompting.

"Oh, dear, I'm not sure I should be worrying you at a time like this. It may be nothing, but as I've told the police now… There was a man watching your house. I noticed him first on Monday. He was sitting in a car parked across the street. Stayed there for hours. Same thing on Tuesday. I'm sure it was the same man. He was wearing a baseball cap on Tuesday, pulled down to disguise himself, I suppose. He was 'casing the joint,' I think they call it." She nodded, pleased with herself for finding the apt term.

"What did Geraldine say?" Thomas asked.

Ellie looked surprised. "Well, I don't remember. I think she thanked me. She was in a hurry to be off to work."

"And you've not seen the man since?"

"No." She sounded disappointed. "Oh, this morning there was someone parked in the same spot, but not him. I think it was Geraldine's friend, I don't know her name. Did she stop by?"

"Mmm." *Diana*. Thomas didn't say it. He stood back to indicate ushering Ellie out. She took the hint.

"Three-fifty degrees for thirty minutes," she called as he shut the door behind her.

Thomas returned to his study with a renewed sense of purpose. He exited the document he'd been pretending to revise, and, using Geraldine's password, he logged into her email account. Was it too early to receive an answer to the message he'd sent in her name?

Chapter 7

Marco read the last page, closed the novel, and placed it on the cafeteria table. He rested his hand on the book as if in benediction. After some effort, he had at last got the hang of Dickens. Yes, the heroine was clueless and naive, and the other characters overdrawn and exaggerated, but they leaped out of their nineteenth-century English setting into his world, making him see both the homeless men at the mission and the privileged students at the university with fresh eyes. His satisfaction at finishing *Bleak House* was bittersweet, however. He could not discuss his epiphany with his English professor: she was dead.

Someone approached the table and stood over him. It took a moment to recognize Aubrey: a bright orange knitted hat was pulled down to her eyebrows and she wore an oversized camo jacket and heavy army boots.

"Hi," she said. "Wanna come to a party tonight?"

"Thanks, but I have to work," Marco replied. He was puzzled at why she would seek him out. Except for the morning they found Professor Harmon, they had never spoken.

"It won't get started 'til late. Come after work."

"No, sorry, I can't." He was about to explain that he worked all night, when she grabbed his hand, produced a Sharpie, and wrote a number on his palm.

"Call me. Anytime." Aubrey smiled—more of a

leer—and stomped off. Marco stared at the number, wondering how hard it would be to wash off the ink.

He had time to stop by the halfway house and pick up another book before his shift at the mission started. He was lucky to have secured a place for those in recovery and newly released prisoners with nowhere else to go. The converted motel was clean and bright. There was always someone to talk to who understood his situation. If he wanted privacy, he could retreat to his unit. Marco would have to move on soon when his allotted year was up. He wasn't hopeful about finding a place he could afford on his own, but he was reluctant to move in with roommates. Perhaps something would turn up.

Arriving at the shelter, Marco was pleased to see that Joan and Bill were the volunteers on duty for the night. The couple, now in their seventies, were faithful Catholics and had a history of service and activism that went back decades. He liked to hear them talk about their time in El Salvador and Nicaragua during the civil wars of the seventies, and more recent peaceful protests at Army recruiting stations and nuclear bases in the States. But there would be no opportunity to chat until lights-out when things quietened down.

Joan was cleaning up in the kitchen, while Marco circled the room picking up stray cups and plates left after dinner. He saw Bill over in a corner, seated opposite another man, their foreheads almost touching and their hands clasped together between them. The other man was Jesús, the guy who'd thrown up a few nights ago. Marco had not noticed him come in, and he went over to the sign-in sheet to check for his name. As he suspected, there was no Jesús listed. He must have snuck in after dinner like last time.

Curious, Marco wandered back toward the two men, a neatly shorn white head close to dark shoulder-length locks with a greasy sheen. He didn't want to interrupt them, since they seemed so intent on what they were discussing. As he neared, he heard a foreign language: Bill was doing most of the talking, with Jesús making short responses. Spanish, Marco thought. Then he recognized a phrase: *Ave Maria*. They were praying together in Latin. Who spoke Latin anymore? Even the Roman Catholic Church had abandoned the dead language. Marco could hardly wait until after lights-out when he might be able to find out more from Bill about the mystery guest.

But when Bill entered the office, he seemed troubled, so Marco waited until he had poured a cup of coffee and exchanged a few words with his wife before he questioned him.

"I saw you talking to Jesús," Marco said. "Any idea why he's so reluctant to put his name on the sign-in sheet? He arrives after dinner and leaves quickly in the morning."

"Ah, Jesús…" Bill looked over at Joan. "Do you remember, dear, the trail up to Santa Ana?"

Joan nodded. "It was so cold, and the children had no coats. That was forty years ago, Bill. It's all different now, surely?"

Marco continued to wait. He knew pressing for concise answers would be counterproductive. These two loved to tell their stories their own way; truth would emerge in its own good time.

"Not so different, apparently," Bill continued, turning to Marco. "During the civil war, we helped refugees escape north from El Salvador to Guatemala. The safest way was to avoid the roads in the valleys and keep to the hills. Santa Ana is one of a string of volcanos. The locals think the Devil lives there, that it's the entrance to Hell. The legends kept *los maderos* away."

"*Los maderos*?" asked Marco.

"The cops—thugs mostly. They could be bribed, but the poor people we worked with had no money." Bill sipped his coffee. "The end of the civil war did not end corruption. Guns and drugs: it's a never-ending loop. Now the gangs have control. And the refugees keep coming."

"So Jesús is a refugee from El Salvador?"

"Yes…" Bill's hesitancy told Marco there was something more.

"You were speaking in Latin with him. He must be an educated man," Marco probed. "I thought ordinary Catholics didn't use Latin anymore. Is he a priest?"

"Not exactly," Bill replied. "Have you ever heard of the *Cofradia*?"

Joan gasped and gave her husband an alarmed look.

Marco leaned forward. This sounded interesting.

"No. What's the *Cofradia*?"

"It's a secret society within the Catholic Church. It means "fraternity" and was founded during the Cold War to protect Catholics being persecuted under communism in eastern Europe, China and elsewhere."

Joan interrupted, her voice taut with anger. "But what started as a mission to help and protect became a tool of dictators and murderers—"

"Hush, dear, not so loud." Bill made a calming gesture with his hands. "Yes, it's true. In Central America, the right-wing governments used the society to hunt out dissidents, especially in the Church: priests and others who wanted to help the poor, who preached Liberation Theology. People like us," he ended quietly.

"It's why we had to leave our work in El Salvador and come home," Joan added.

"So Jesús is escaping the *Cofradia*?" This sounded to Marco like a movie plot. He had no idea what Liberation Theology was and only a dim knowledge of Central American politics. What could any of it have to do with their own sleepy little town?

"Yes, in a way." Bill glanced nervously at Joan, worried she might erupt again. "Jesús was recruited into the *Cofradia* when he was a teenager at seminary—that's where he learned Latin, by the way—but he became disgusted with their tactics and wanted to leave. Now they're hunting him. He knows too much. Regimes have changed and the *Cofradia* has been dissolved, at least officially. The men who carried out the killings years ago are still around, some of them in high positions. Jesús is afraid."

"Then we must help him," announced Joan.

****

The party was not as much fun as Aubrey had hoped. She smoked some weed and drank a few beers, enough to loosen her up. The music was loud and she had to pull out her phone a few times to see if there was a call from Marco: she'd never hear the ring tone over the noise. A neighbor must have complained, because at one a.m. she saw the flashing lights of a police car outside. Six or seven guys were hurrying out the back door and she followed them.

"Y'all can come back to my place," said a kid who didn't look old enough for high school, let alone college.

He was bombed. "My parents are out of town."

Aubrey didn't know any of the group, but no one said anything when she tagged along for a couple of blocks to a neat Victorian set back from the street behind a well-kept lawn. She drank more beer, and some vodka. A poker game started. She didn't know how to play so she checked her phone again and crashed down on a sofa to watch. Someone handed around some pills but no one offered her any and she was too lethargic to object. Her thoughts meandered back to Marco. He was hot. He was cool, too: mysterious, older than most of the other students, with more experience. That made him cool. And hot too...

When Aubrey woke, she was alone. It was beginning to get light. The room smelt of marijuana and spilled beer. She needed a bathroom. When she found the right door, she recoiled—vomit all over the floor—and ended up peeing in the bushes at the side of the house. She still had her phone and car keys but was bummed that she couldn't find her hat. It was her favorite: bright orange with a Clemson University logo. She'd stolen it from a previous boyfriend as a trophy when he dumped her. The hat might be at the first party house, but when she'd made her way back there she didn't go inside, just got into her car and drove home.

Standing inside the front door, she heard a noise like a dog whimpering in pain.

"Jeremy! Come here, boy!" she called. The dachshund mix trotted out of the kitchen, tail a-wagging, and she bent to fondle his ears. The noise continued. It came from upstairs, her mother's room. Aubrey wanted nothing more than to collapse into bed and sleep. She'd miss her morning class, but so what? She'd borrow

Marco's notes. First, she had to stop that noise. She nudged open Hannah's bedroom door.

"Aubrey! It's awful! I've been hacked!"

Hannah was a mess. Her hair hung in damp strings around a blotched face. Snot and tears smeared her cheeks. The noise started again.

"Get a grip, Ma, and stop yowling! What happened?"

"I've been hacked!" Hannah repeated, pointing at her phone lying on top of the duvet. Aubrey picked it up and stared at the screen.

"Shit, Mom, it's you!" Aubrey barked out a laugh that turned into a gasp.

"No! Well, yes, it's my face but someone's put it on…" Hannah waved a hand at the phone, unable to describe out loud what Aubrey was looking at: a naked female body gyrating sexily with her mother's carefully made-up and tilt-posed face above it.

"That's some pair of boobs," Aubrey blew air out in admiration. "Definitely not yours," she added flatly.

"I know that! Who could have done this to me? It's awful!"

"Well, I told you to get off Facebook. Haven't you heard of Russian bots?" Aubrey was fixated on the manufactured image.

"No, you didn't tell me, just like you didn't tell me about the kickboxing class," Hannah replied with acerbity. "And why would a Russian bot come after me?"

"Nah, it's probably one of your Facebook friends."

"They're my *friends*!" Hannah howled.

Aubrey sat down on the bed and flicked through a few screens.

"Mom, do you actually *know* all these people?"

"No, but they know me. They asked to be my friend—"

"And you accepted their friend request without checking? Christ! And look, your posts are set on public! Are you completely stupid or what?"

"Oh, yes." A hint of shame crept into Hannah's voice. "I switched to public for that lost puppy post and forgot to switch it back to private. Can you help, Aubrey, sweetie? Can you delete it?" She was pleading now.

Aubrey threw the device onto the bed.

"Done. I've deleted it. But, Mom, you know it's still out there. It's been circulating for hours on who knows how many people's phones. You. Are. Screwed." Aubrey cackled. "Well, maybe you will be, after this!"

Chapter 8

Cindy's landscaping contract with St. Xavier's required one more day of clean-up work before year's end. Until a few years ago, the parish had relied on volunteers to keep the landscaped half-acre between the church and the rectory tidy, but the congregation had dwindled, and most of the remaining members were elderly, so Cindy now mowed the lawn and pruned the bushes. Her task this morning was to cut back dead perennials and clear leaves that had blown onto the curving paths linking the two buildings and a third known as the Old School at the rear of the gardens. Recent rains had made the fallen leaves slippery. If it had been left to her, Cindy would have mounded them as mulch around the tree trunks and shrubs to provide winter habitat for insects, but Father Odell wanted her to remove them, and he was paying.

Cindy parked the truck in the alley that ran behind the Old School, and carried her tools around the corner of the building to start work in the gardens. The structure hadn't been used as a school for years; it was partially boarded up, and the double doors were secured with a chain and padlock.

It took Cindy about an hour to cut back withered plants and bag the detritus. Before firing up the leaf blower, she decided to duck into the church to make sure there was no service in process—the gas-powered blower made an awful noise. When she'd called Father Odell the day before to let him know her work plans, he'd said he would be away at a diocesan conference, so she was a little surprised to find the church unlocked.

"Just mail me the invoice or put it under the door at the church office," he'd told her. The rectory, where three priests and their housekeeper once lived, now housed the office and meeting rooms, with just a small apartment on the top floor reserved for the lone parish priest.

Cindy crept into the sanctuary, breathing in the smell of incense. The gloom was pierced by a few candles—the electric, ever-burning variety—in front of side chapels. A couple sat in the back pew of the nave, talking in hushed voices. Cindy coughed to alert them to her presence, and they swung around in unison to stare at her. They were both gray-haired and stoop-shouldered, their faces gleaming ghostly in the dim light. She wondered for a moment if they were homeless, but their clothes were neat and clean.

"Excuse me. I wondered if there was a service about to begin. I've got some noisy machinery outside and I don't want to disturb you." Cindy also spoke in the hushed tone she thought was required in church.

"No, no service. We were just…uh…talking," the man responded. He seemed uncertain; perhaps her sudden appearance had startled him.

His wife—Cindy assumed they were married, they looked like a matched pair—spoke in a firmer voice. "We're just finishing here. You go ahead. It won't bother us."

Cindy left the church, put on her noise-cancelling earphones, and started work. Although blowing leaves was her least favorite part of the job, it did allow time for her mind to wander. The scent of incense and the dimness of the church had reminded her of her youthful years spent backpacking around Europe. She had been raised without religion, but the grand cathedrals and even the tiny mountain chapels stirred her. She'd passed hours in their interiors, thinking about the many generations of worshipers who had knelt there. Within their ancient walls, she found a serenity that calmed her usual restlessness, the urge that had driven her to shake off family and friends and find a new identity on another continent. Eventually, she found her way to a farm in Devon—a commune, it would have been called in an earlier decade. The pair in St. Xavier's reminded her of the old hippie couple who had established the farm community. Although in their seventies, they worked as hard as the younger members to make the enterprise sustainable. There, Cindy learned the basics of agriculture and horticulture, along with other skills like herbal medicine and motor vehicle maintenance.

She wondered whether the farm had survived. She had lost touch with the other residents after she returned to the States to look after her father in late-stage colon cancer. But the values she had learned living in the community stuck with her: love of nature, and the patience to listen for its rhythms. Patience with human nature too, empathy and the ability to offer unprejudiced support. Cindy would always be a loner, but that didn't mean she couldn't make connections with others; she just didn't want to live with them.

She returned the blower to the truck in the alley and checked on Josie. The dog was supposed to be on guard but was curled up asleep in the passenger seat.

"You lazy good-for-nothing." Cindy chuckled, opening the door to fondle the pup, now stretching and yawning. Then, as if remembering his role, he started barking. Cindy glanced up. The couple from the church was coming down the alley. The man carried two grocery sacks and the woman had what looked like blankets. They turned into the church property without seeing her, half-hidden as she leaned into the cab.

Cindy made a couple of trips to retrieve bags of leaves and load them in the truck bed for delivery to the green recycling center. Returning to the gardens one last time to check around for any forgotten tools, she sensed something was amiss. She stood on the grass and looked around. It took a moment to notice that the chain and padlock securing the double doors to the Old School were now lying on the steps outside. Perhaps the old couple had opened up the derelict building to store some items. Cindy was uneasy. On the one hand, she wasn't paid to be the church custodian. It was none of her business who went in and out of the buildings. On the other, she knew the priest was away, and she had no idea whether the couple had anything to do with the parish or had permission to be here.

She climbed the steps to the doors and listened, hearing sounds of movement inside. She touched one of the doors and it opened inward, creaking a little. Now she could hear low voices. Entering a dark vestibule, she made out three doors, presumably to the classrooms. The center door was ajar. *None of my business,* she thought again, even as she pushed the door open and walked in.

Three figures were bent over their tasks. At one side of the room, the woman Cindy had seen in the church was unpacking groceries and stacking them against the wall. The man was spreading out a sleeping bag along the opposite wall. Beyond them, a third figure with his back to Cindy was cleaning off a table. At her entrance, all three stood upright and turned toward her, mouths open in surprise.

"Jesús!" She had no difficulty in recognizing him. His face had been in her thoughts several times since the night she had cared for him at the homeless shelter. He was still wearing the University of California sweatshirt from the storeroom there.

A rapid exchange in Spanish ensued, of which Cindy could understand nothing. After a pause, the old man stepped forward with his hand outstretched.

"Hi, I'm Bill, and this is my wife Joan. I understand you know our friend here from the mission. We volunteer there too."

They shook hands. Cindy was aware that the other two had not moved toward her and Joan's expression was suspicious bordering on hostile.

"I saw that the lock had been removed." Cindy gestured behind her at the doors. "I didn't think this building was used for anything. Is Jesús living here? It can't be very comfortable. Is there even electricity or running water?" She was on the point of asking whether Father Odell knew of the arrangement, but that seemed a touch too officious.

Joan spoke up. "He'll be quite comfortable. We're looking after him, and bringing him what he needs."

Cindy looked around the room. Besides the wooden table—perhaps the former teacher's desk—there were a few broken chairs and desks piled in a corner. The lower windows were boarded up, but light penetrated through a row of clerestory windows beneath the high ceiling—

enough to show that every surface was thick with dust. "You know, there's room at the mission, and he can get a shower and a hot meal there."

"But he'll be safer here," Joan responded. Bill shot her a warning glare, and she turned back to the grocery bags. Jesús asked a question in Spanish and Bill replied in the same language.

Cindy waited. Someone would explain the situation to her. If she pushed, walls would come up, and she would be on the other side of them.

"You're right," Bill said. "The water's been turned off. I couldn't find the shut-off. Perhaps you can help. Then he'd have a functioning toilet, at least."

Cindy smiled at Jesús and he rewarded her in kind. She remembered how his face transformed from tragic to beautiful with a smile. "I'll give it a try. Where's the bathroom?"

Bill and Cindy spent twenty minutes following pipes along grimy walls and into spider-webbed cupboards before they located the shut-off valve for the water. They tested that the toilet flushed and water ran through the taps before returning to the classroom where Joan and Jesús had finished setting up camp.

"Look," Cindy said. She had refrained from asking Bill questions while they solved the water problem, but now she felt she was due some answers. "Father Odell will be back tomorrow and he's sure to notice something's going on. What are you going to tell him?"

"We're not worried about Father Odell. He's a good man and he knows us. We've been members at St. Xavier's for years," Joan answered. "It's not him Jesús is afraid of."

"Is he undocumented? Because I have friends

who—"

Bill cut Cindy off. "That's not the problem. The *migra* aren't after him. It's much more dangerous than that." He paused, pondering how much to reveal. Then, with a sigh, he gestured for Jesús to approach. "This man—" placing an arm around Jesús' shoulders "—is on the run from an organization of assassins called the *Cofradia*. He knows their identities, and the location of a document that reveals their crimes, or at least he's been told who has the document. The members of this organization will not hesitate to kill to preserve their secrets. The mission is not a safe hiding place."

Joan gripped Cindy's arm. "Can we trust you to say nothing? We're going to speak to Father Odell when he gets back tomorrow. We're confident he'll offer Jesús sanctuary. It's been the Church's duty for centuries to protect the persecuted."

Cindy nodded slowly as she took all this in. Joan and Bill seemed sincere, and while her faith in Jesús's essential decency had no evidentiary basis, her intuition on this point was strong. "What can I do to help? He can't stay hidden here forever. What's the plan?"

There was no plan. The activist networks Joan and Bill knew from thirty years ago no longer existed. They had no trusted contacts in the media or any current connections with people who might have the power to help Jesús. Their only hope had been to get in touch with the man who had been entrusted with the document, but that proved a dead end: the phone number Jesús had was disconnected, and they only had a first name—Gerry— which was untraceable, perhaps deliberately so.

"Very sorry," said Jesús. He shrugged and smiled his transforming smile.

Chapter 9

"What work experience do you have?" Mr. Karapoulas asked.

His expectation that applicants would come armed with a neatly printed resume—the norm when he hired for his accounting practice—had proved unrealistic. He was learning that a part-time sales position in a small greeting card and gift shop did not attract that kind of candidate. The shop was his wife's project. He had wanted to close it when she fell ill, but she pleaded with him to keep it going. Hoping the store's continued existence would motivate her to continue battling the cancer, he had given in, but he was finding it hard going. Although he was supposed to be retired from the firm he had founded and their sons now ran, some older clients still required his personal attention. He compromised by advertising for an assistant to cover afternoons at the shop.

Aubrey's brow furrowed with concentration. "Um...babysitting," she responded. "Oh, and I helped my mom out at the cat café."

"The cat café?" Mr. Karapoulas looked puzzled.

"Yeah, a café my mom started where you pet cats and have them on your lap and stuff while you drink a coffee.... Or tea, if you like," she added.

"Did you serve food?" The accountant was having a hard time picturing the establishment.

"Nah, just drinks, but the Health Department shut us down anyway—fleas, and something you catch from litter boxes with a Latin name."

"Oh." Mr. Karapoulas searched for other questions to ask. This girl, even without any meaningful experience, was an improvement on the only other applicant he had interviewed: a middle-aged woman who stank of cigarettes and announced she couldn't work weekends "because of my nerves," and couldn't lift more than ten pounds "because of my back." So what if the girl turned up in skinny jeans and an oversized sweater? His expectation of a business suit and pantyhose was probably another relic of a bygone age. At least there were no visible tattoos.

"The hours are not a problem then? Two until six, Tuesday through Saturday? Can I count on you?"

Aubrey nodded her head vigorously. The accountant considered while Aubrey gazed around the store, taking in the varied displays. *Like a kid in a candy store*, he thought. The image, conjuring up his own youth and innocence, decided him.

"All right then. Let me go through the rules—no shirt, no shoes, no service. Not that that's a problem this time of year. Customers aren't allowed to bring food and drinks into the store, and if they break something they have to pay for it. I'll be back at 5:45 p.m. every day to close out the register and lock up. Oh, and one more thing—I don't want you on the phone while you're working. Big Brother is watching you!" He smiled and nodded his head toward the security camera mounted high on the wall behind the counter. It wasn't connected to a monitor, but he saw no need to tell the girl that.

Aubrey didn't get the reference. "So your brother

works here too?"

"What? No." He sighed, feeling old. "Let me show you how to use the cash register and card reader."

\*\*\*\*

Dave had a twenty-hour layover before trucking the next load to Arizona, and he was determined not to get into trouble this time. He arrived late at the depot. After checking in, he slept for nine hours in his cab. Then he whiled away some time on his phone. Joanne wasn't picking up, so he left her a couple of texts. He hoped things were all right between them; she hadn't mentioned Hannah again after the trick she played on her Facebook page, and she'd given him a big smooch when he left.

Hunger drove him out at two in the afternoon. He'd seen a "breakfast all day" neon sign on his way in. He headed up the hill away from the waterfront to find the diner, reasoning the lunch hour rush had ended and it wasn't the kind of place Hannah frequented anyway. The waitress—a scrawny bleached blonde with an inch of gray roots showing—told him to sit where he liked. He chose a booth away from the windows. There were only a couple of other customers in the place.

"What can I get you?" The waitress stood with a hip thrust out and a pencil poised over her pad.

"Two eggs up, bacon and hash-browns, white toast and coffee, please, Liz." Dave smiled up at her. She wasn't his type—too thin—but the habit of being friendly to waitresses was ingrained, and her name was embroidered on her uniform. "Oh, and a large orange juice. Gotta stay healthy!"

She smiled back and sashayed off to fix his order. He took his time over the meal. By the time Liz returned to fill his coffee cup a third time, he was the only customer left.

"Can I get you anything else?" she asked. Dave noticed that the top two buttons of her uniform were now undone. A come-on? Not that there was much to reveal.

"Just the check, please." He averted his eyes, proud of himself for resisting. "Oh, maybe you can tell me where I could buy a gift, something nice for my wife?"

The waitress ripped the check off her pad with unnecessary force and slapped it on the table. "Downtown's that way," she jerked her head up the hill, the opposite direction to where Dave had come from. "You'll find shops there. You can pay at the counter when you leave."

He paid and headed out into the gathering dusk. He'd walked about a half-mile and was wondering how much farther downtown was when he spotted a shop on the other side of the street called the Mermaid's Closet. The window display promised "greeting cards, gifts and tourist memorabilia." He crossed and entered.

****

Aubrey was surprised to find she quite enjoyed the job at the Mermaid's Closet. Few customers penetrated this part of town where the boutiques and restaurants gave way to warehouses and gas stations. She suspected the receipts Mr. K. totaled up each evening failed to cover her wages, but that was not her problem. She was left with plenty of time to browse the greeting cards— some of them were laugh-out-loud funny. The poems in the sympathy and friendship cards were cheesy, but she liked to read them aloud, trying on different accents and voices—maybe she'd be an actress one day. Her favorite thing was rearranging the figurines and toys into semi-pornographic scenarios: a crystal angel kneeling in prayer at the crotch of Sasquatch, or a soft toy puppy astride a reclining mermaid ornament. Every afternoon when Aubrey came to work, Mr. K had sorted them back into boring forward-facing rows. He never said anything, so she kept on doing it. By day two, she'd worked out that the no-phone rule could be ignored without any adverse consequences. The four hours passed pleasantly, *and* she had money to spend without having to raid her mother's purse or submit to an interrogation about what she wanted the cash for.

The doorbell jangled. Aubrey looked up from her device to see a big man with dark hair, beard and a leather jacket enter the store. Instead of wandering the aisles, he made straight for the counter.

"Can I help you find something, sir?" Aubrey had the patter down.

The man loomed over her and she caught a whiff of spicy cologne. He reached inside his jacket and she instinctively flinched. She'd watched cop shows on TV.

"You seen dis man?" The accent was Hispanic. He placed a photograph of another dark-haired man—this one with hollow cheekbones and a cross hanging around his neck—on the counter in front of her.

"I don't think so." The door jangled again; two customers in the shop at once—a record. The newcomer was hidden behind the jewelry display, seeming to take his or her time browsing the wares.

The man at the counter jabbed the photo with a beringed finger. "You sure?"

Aubrey felt nervous. Mr. K's cursory training had failed to cover dealing with a threatening customer. She was relieved when the other customer appeared to have made a selection and approached with a pair of earrings in his hand. He stood at the counter and glanced sideways at the photo.

"Yeah, I've seen him around, maybe a week ago."

The other man and Aubrey spoke at the same time.

"Where? Where you see him?"

"Hey! You're Dave, the asshole who ditched my mom!"

Dave stumbled back a step. "Oh, hi…er, Amber. I've been on the road, meaning to get in touch…"

The bearded Latino grabbed Dave by the front of his pea jacket. "Where is he?"

"Easy now! I saw him across from the Mission, down by the waterfront. He was maybe waiting to get in."

The other man released him, and Dave edged toward the door. Aubrey leaned forward, eyes narrowed. "You gonna pay for those earrings?"

Dave came back to the counter and threw a twenty down, then made his escape, followed by Leather Jacket Guy. Aubrey rang up the sale, smirking as she put the bill in the cash register. The earrings were priced at $12.99. Mr. K would be pleased.

****

Marco stood near the entrance doors, greeting the men in line signing into the shelter for the night. Most were regulars who knew the ropes. They shuffled along in silence. A hot meal would loosen them up and the noise level would soon increase. Marco kept an eye out for newbies, the ones who glanced around suspiciously or tried to avoid writing their name on the sheet. These, he guided forward as he explained the routine and answered questions. At the same time, he counted heads, knowing that if he let in more men than the shelter had

91

beds for, fights would break out. Tonight, it looked like there would be room for everyone.

While these routine tasks occupied the surface of his attention, worry nagged at Marco's thoughts. In less than a month, he would have to move on from the halfway house, having completed his subsidized year of recovery there. He had followed up on some ads for roommates in the student newspaper. The opportunities he could afford meant sharing a room in a crowded house where he knew he would be surrounded by hard-drinking party animals. Although he'd gained confidence in his sobriety, he was unsure if he could withstand that kind of constant temptation. He was on a waiting list for a room in the freshman dormitory building. Availability would depend on enough students giving up their studies and moving home midway through the academic year. Even if that happened, Marco didn't relish the thought of being surrounded by a bunch of kids. His life experiences had given him a maturity beyond his twenty-six years. He left a voicemail message for his social worker confiding his concerns, but it seemed even she was running out of time for him. She texted him a schedule of Alcoholics Anonymous meetings, and wished him good luck with three exclamation points.

Before going back to help the other workers with the food line, Marco stepped outside to check for stragglers. He stood breathing in the chill damp air, mulling over his problems. Perhaps he would go back to AA; Christmas was coming up, always a tricky time for the addict. If he did become homeless, he wondered if he could keep his job at the Mission. At least the commute would be short. Allowing himself a grin at this thought, he turned to go inside when a figure separated from the shadows. Marco had barely time to assess the man as not homeless—casual but fashionable clothing and well-groomed—before the man was toe-to-toe with him. Startled, Marco stepped backward, and, because he was embarrassed at his retreat, he spoke in a rougher tone than usual.

"You're too late. You have to be here by six."

The man smiled but remained intimidatingly close. He was tall and muscular, with dark hair and beard, a dark sweater topped by a leather jacket. Marco caught the scent of cologne.

"I search for friend," the man said, pulling out a photograph. "Him. He here, yes?"

Marco recognized the face in the photo. He shrugged. "No, he's not here."

"I come inside and see?"

Marco did not like this stranger. His brief time in jail and on the streets had given him an instinct for danger. Danger oozed from this man's perfumed pores. "Nope. We don't allow non-guests in. You should leave."

"You have a list of dese 'guests'?" he replied with a sneer, pulling something from his jacket pocket and pushing it toward Marco's face. Marco recoiled; it was a roll of bills—twenties, he thought. "Jus' let me see de list."

"No. Go now or I'll call the police. They have a patrol car parked a block away." This was true, although Marco had never had occasion to summon it. He suspected the cops parked there for their break; it was across from an all-night diner. Before the man could respond, he went inside and locked the door behind him. He watched the stranger leave, wondering how much money was in that roll of bills.

Chapter 10

Detective Sergeant Barry Fish leaned back, balancing his chair on two legs. Melinda Deniro had to restrain herself from reaching out to steady him. Although they were far from solving the case, Fish wore a satisfied smile. He had managed to get Melinda officially reassigned—at least temporarily—to the detective squad, doubling its strength. And they were allocated a small conference room as an Ops Center. A whiteboard hung on one wall of the room, cork paneling covered an adjacent wall, and two computer terminals sat on the table that took up most of the space.

Melinda, showing the initiative that Fish had suspected she possessed, had "borrowed" a coffeemaker from the break room, and brought a pound of superior coffee from home to fuel it. Fish was enjoying a mugful of the brew as he teetered, surveying the photograph pinned to the center of the cork: Geraldine Harmon, looking young and eager in her faculty profile portrait.

"So, what have we got so far?" Fish asked, bringing his chair upright and almost—but not quite—spilling his coffee. Melinda recognized a rhetorical question when she heard one. She waited, hovering over the various files strewn across the tabletop. "Geraldine Harmon's body was found in her office at 10:10 a.m. on Wednesday, November 30. She entered the room at 8:30 a.m. and time of death is pegged at between 9 and 9:30

a.m. There were no obvious signs of a struggle, except slight *ante mortem* bruising on the left side of her neck."

Melinda whipped out a photograph from a file and pinned it beneath Geraldine's portrait. The autopsy report had at last arrived. The photo showed her head and upper torso, a faint purple mark above the collarbone.

"Blood and stomach content analyses reveal the presence of Trazadone," Fish continued. Melinda extracted another photo from a second file: a picture of the contents of the Harmons' medicine cabinet. This was taken by the detective on his phone during the execution of a search warrant at the deceased's home. A black Sharpie circle on the photograph drew attention to a vial of Trazadone 50 mg tablets. "Professor Harmon's primary care doctor confirms the drug was prescribed to her in June for anxiety and depression. It's also used off-label as a sleep aid."

While Melinda pinned the medicine cabinet photo to the board, Fish pulled the autopsy report toward him and reviewed it. " 'The amount of Trazadone ingested might have made the deceased drowsy but she would still be conscious,' " he read aloud. " 'Also present in the bloodstream was an alkaloid extract from a plant commonly known as Angel's Trumpet found only in certain rain forest areas at the headwaters of the Amazon. Used by shamans to induce a dreamlike or hallucinogenic state, this alkaloid can be lethal'—listen to this, Melinda—'if taken in combination with other sedatives or narcotics, *such as Trazadone*!' "

"How does Dr. Khan think the…alka-thing got into the professor?" Melinda asked. She had not yet had a chance to do more than glance through the autopsy report.

"Injection. When he went back over the body with magnification, he found an injection site in her lower leg. A very fine needle was used. The report leaves a lot of questions unanswered, though. Could the alkaloid injection have been self-administered? A bizarre suicide? That assumes she knew about the interaction with Trazadone, which is unlikely as it took our Medical Examiner days of research to track it down as the cause of death."

"It also assumes she took the Trazadone herself, that it wasn't slipped into her coffee by someone else." This was the most fun Melinda had had since she joined the police.

"Okay, I think we can rule out suicide for the moment." Barry turned his attention to the blank whiteboard. "Let's start filling in some names and thinking about motive, means and opportunity."

"Could it have been an accident?" Melinda suggested.

"What...she accidentally fell onto a hypodermic syringe filled with a rare plant extract from the Amazon? Nah! Even if the person who injected her didn't mean to kill her, just reduce her resistance, like a date-rape drug, it did result in her death. We'll leave it to the prosecutor to decide the charges, but it's a homicide of some sort."

*He's enjoying this too,* Melinda thought. *Homicide makes him happy.* She picked up a marker and walked around the table to stand poised in front of the whiteboard. She knew which name Barry would tell her to write first, but she waited for him to speak.

"I kinda like the husband for this, but we should keep an open mind."

Melinda wrote "Thomas Harmon, husband" at the

top right of the board.

"He hasn't admitted to grabbing his wife by the neck, but the timing's right according to the doc—an hour before death, breakfast time," Fish continued.

"But that didn't kill her, or contribute to her death." Melinda felt obliged to be the devil's advocate, even if Barry shot down her theories. After all, he'd told her to keep an open mind.

"Goes to motive," he replied. "How 'bout this? They fight at home over breakfast. He grabs her throat. She's upset so takes some Trazadone to calm herself down before she leaves for work. He follows her, enters her office the back way via the alley, and injects her." Looking at Melinda's face told him what she thought of his theory. "Okay, I get it. Who has a hypo of rare plant extract lying around? And if he's mad enough to try and strangle her at breakfast, he's more likely to bash her over the head if he wants to finish the job. The injection shows planning and preparation, not a crime of passion."

"What about the friend Diana Latour's evidence?" Melinda reminded him. "She said Geraldine was anxious about something, thought she was being gaslighted." She wrote "Diana Latour, friend" next to Thomas's name.

"The gaslighting thing points back at the husband. It's clear he and Diana didn't get along. She wants us to suspect him."

"But she also told us that Geraldine was worried she'd lost a manuscript or something. That could be quite separate. Whose manuscript? Maybe it was important enough for the author to come after her." Melinda wrote "missing manuscript?" under Diana's name.

"Hmm. The answers might be in the professor's missing laptop. How are we doing with getting access to her dot-e-d-u email account?" Barry asked.

"I'll follow it up, as well as the cell phone call records." Melinda made herself a reminder, then paused, tapping her pencil against her chin. "The man the neighbor spotted watching the Harmon house—could he be the author of the manuscript?"

Barry chuckled. "You can put it on the board if you like, but it's a huge leap from a sighting by nosy neighbor to being a homicidal author."

Melinda's cheeks reddened, but she wrote "Ellie Posner, neighbor" at the top of the whiteboard, and "man in car" underneath.

There was a knock at the door to the conference room. Before Melinda could move to answer it, the door opened to reveal the captain. He stood on the threshold, like a reluctant swimmer at the edge of the pool. Before speaking, he peered at the photos and the writing on the whiteboard.

"Solved it yet, Fish?"

"Working on it, sir," Barry replied. He remained seated in a relaxed pose, smiling up at his boss, but his eyes turned hard.

The captain taught a class at the academy on "Modern Policing." He required everyone in the Department to submit a complicated spreadsheet each week showing in detail how their time was spent and the results obtained. From this data, he calculated a "resolution score." Fish had complained about and resisted the spreadsheet practice. Not only did it take hours to complete—time better spent looking for criminals—but it equated issuing a parking ticket with arresting a murderer as a "resolution." The detective had the worst resolution score in the Department, and the captain never missed an opportunity to remind him of that fact. Fish knew Melinda's secondment and the Ops Center were the result of pressure from the Chief of Police; the captain didn't like either action. The chief and Barry went back a long way—both were old-fashioned coppers who relied on instinct rather than data, and cut corners once in a while if they thought it was justified. But the chief was due to retire soon and had ceded most day-to-day management to the captain.

"Yes, well, it's been over a week, and no result, so I'm thinking of handing the case over to the County. They have the manpower—" he glanced over at Melinda— "I mean, *the resources* for a long-term investigation. We just had a report of another robbery. I want you both on it pronto!"

"Yes, sir!" Fish wanted to give a mock salute but thought the gesture might be too obviously sarcastic. "We'll handle it at once. But there's some follow-up on the Harmon case we need to get squared away before we hand it over to County. I'm sure you don't want us to hand over paperwork that shows a half-assed investigation. It wouldn't reflect well on the Department. By the way, what's the robbery?"

The captain looked embarrassed. "Bicycle taken from outside a local coffee shop last night. Owner just reported it. Okay, tie up those loose ends on the Harmon case, but I want results by the end of the week, or the case goes to County!" He turned and stalked off, leaving the door open.

Fish scowled at the space. "What was missing from the scene?" He tipped his chair back again.

"'Scuse me?" Melinda was puzzled: the captain had clearly said a bike was taken.

"The professor's laptop and phone were taken, presumably by whoever injected her with Angel's Trumpet. But her coffee cup was missing too. The receptionist at the college said she always brought her own coffee to work in the morning. We need to follow that up. Did she bring it from home or buy it on the way?" He grinned. "Maybe we can kill two birds with one stone and ask about the bike at the same time." Turning serious, he continued. "Find out whether the trash dumpster in the alley behind Harmon's office has been emptied. Put a hold on it if it hasn't. We need to go through it. Talk to the neighbor again to get a better description of the man she saw outside the Harmon house. In fact, do a canvas of the other neighbors too. Open-ended questions, mind. Oh, and we should interview her colleagues."

"Academic rivalry turned violent?" Melinda suggested as she scribbled down the to-do items.

"Maybe. 'The Missing Manuscript' sounds like an Agatha Christie novel, but I suppose it could provide a motive for one of those intellectual types." Barry paused. Not meeting Melinda's eye, he said, "I think I'll re-interview Ms. Latour. She seems to know the victim well and a lot about her marriage. In a more relaxed setting, she might come up with important details."

*And she's very attractive,* Melinda thought, but all she said was "I just don't see how we can do all this by the end of the week."

"Oh, don't worry about the captain." The detective smiled. "County won't take over this case. They're much too busy breaking the bicycle theft ring."

\*\*\*\*

Hannah was determined to revive the book club.

"I think it would be so good for Tommy. He's completely isolated himself since Gerry died. I'm worried about his mental health." She had called Maisie first with an ulterior motive: had her friend, an avid social media user, seen the salacious video before it was deleted? Hannah wouldn't raise the subject directly, but she thought Maisie might be unable to resist saying something about it.

"Absolutely! I tried to drop off some flowers and that wonderful book on grief recovery—you know the one. It was so helpful after our sweet doggie died—but he wouldn't answer the door, although I'm certain he was home." Maisie's response reassured Hannah that her friend was oblivious about the video.

"I know! I've tried everything: emails, texts, phone calls. But after that first day, he seems to have closed himself off." She didn't add that she had attempted a break-in through the back door, when Thomas had refused to open the front one to her. It sounded a little desperate. "I think this calls for a group intervention. I'm going to call the other book club members and come up with a plan."

Penny and Gus (*not* social media people) were eager to help. Now Hannah just had Diana Latour to call. If *she* had seen the post, Hannah would be mortified with shame. She could only hope that Diana was too sophisticated for social media. She probably spent her online time watching documentaries, or taking virtual philosophy classes from European universities. Anyway, as Diana was such a close friend of Gerry's, she had leverage with Tommy, so the call must be made.

"…I'm worried about his mental health." Hannah rushed through her rationale for a book club intervention, then listened to silence as Diana digested it.

"Mmm. I think that's an excellent idea."

Now it was Hannah's turn to be speechless: Diana Latour approved of her plan!

"But we should wait until after the funeral on Saturday," Diana continued.

"The funeral? What? Where?" Hannah gasped. How could she know nothing about this?

"Yes. The police have released the body, and Geraldine's parents are arriving tomorrow. It's going to be family only, very quiet. I'm sure there'll be a memorial service later for friends and colleagues." Diana took some mischievous pleasure in Hannah's ignorance of the arrangements. She did not add that when she'd called Geraldine's mother, Nancy Riley, to offer condolences—Diana had known the family almost as long as she had known Geraldine—Nancy was racked by rage as well as grief. Thomas had waited three days before informing the parents of Geraldine's death, and then told them nothing of the circumstances. Diana was left to explain what she knew, put them in touch with a funeral home, and arrange a hotel room for their stay in town. Thomas had not even offered to put them up at the house where their daughter had lived.

"Let's talk again after the weekend. I'll call you." Diana disconnected, leaving Hannah with mixed emotions: gratified that Diana had endorsed her idea, but miffed that she had been out of the loop on the funeral.

Diana, however, was content. Hannah, for all her irritating triviality, was a pliable tool who could be employed to further her investigation into the events leading up to Geraldine's death. She was certain that Thomas was responsible in some way.

Chapter 11

Melinda regretted not wearing her uniform. Although delighted to be elevated to the detective ranks, the crisp black outfit with its epaulets and duty belt had endowed her with an authority she missed. She had always appeared young for her age, and now, dressed in jeans and a puffy jacket, she looked like the majority of students wandering around campus. Melinda fingered the police badge in her pocket for comfort.

"You should have called and made an appointment," Anne Summers, the English Department secretary—or Senior Administrative Assistant, her preferred title—scolded. "Professor Hersch is with a student right now."

"I'll wait," Melinda responded, with what was intended as a confident smile. It hadn't been this difficult with Professor Harmon's neighbors. Ellie Posner had provided coffee, cookies, and a much more detailed description of the man in the car than at her first interview.

"He was big and dark-skinned—Mexican or Middle-Eastern or something. And he had a beard, a short one, well-groomed."

"How could you see all that from here?" Melinda glanced toward the sitting room window that faced the street. At least sixty feet of front yard and sidewalk separated the house from any cars parked at the curb.

Mrs. Posner took no offense at Melinda's implied

distrust.

"Oh, no, dear, I was much closer to him! Every morning, as soon as I'm dressed, I go and fetch the *Herald* from the driveway. I don't know why I bother with the subscription, really. There's nothing in it, but I like to scan the obituaries with my coffee. And when I say the driveway, well, half the time I have to go searching in the bushes for it, if it gets delivered at all!" Before Melinda could pull her back on point, the elderly lady rushed on. "I remember that Monday because I had to walk almost to the curb to find the paper, and when I bent down to pick it up, there he was, in this car, just a few feet away from me. He didn't notice me because he was staring at the Harmon house. Very strange, I thought. And even stranger when I saw him the next morning too, parked in the same spot at the same time, about 8:45 a.m. I was a bit farther away on Tuesday—the delivery person had managed to get it halfway up the driveway. Geraldine had already left for work—her car was gone from the driveway. I don't know if her husband was home. He parks in the garage."

"Did you see the man approach the Harmon house?" Melinda asked, as she noted down the information.

"No, I didn't. Of course, I've got better things to do than sit and watch the street all day. He might have knocked on their door, but I don't think so. I would have heard his car door slam, wouldn't I? Anyway, by the time I'd finished my breakfast and the paper, he'd gone."

"And what time was that?"

"Mmm, about 9:30, I think."

Melinda thanked Mrs. Posner for her cooperation and left to canvas the other neighbors. Those who were home were equally generous with offers of refreshment, although they had nothing to add about the man in the car. They were eager to fill out the picture of the Harmon *ménage*: Professor Harmon was "a lovely woman, so kind and friendly," while her husband was "very reserved, a writer, you know, not that I've ever read anything he's published."

Now she was supposed to interview Geraldine's work colleagues before rendezvousing with Barry Fish in the alley to go through the contents of the trash dumpster. She had ascertained that it had not been emptied since the morning of the professor's death. Barry was bringing the protective paper suits and latex gloves.

Melinda glanced at her watch and then at Anne Summers, who shrugged and gave a half-smile that meant, "See? You should have made an appointment." The young detective stood up and wandered away from Ms. Summers' supervision and around the corner into the corridor that led to Geraldine Harmon's office: the crime scene. The nameplate on the first door on the left read "Betsy Pinero." Melinda knocked and was told to enter.

"Hi, I'm Melinda Deniro, a detective with the Police Department. I wonder if you have a few minutes to talk to me about Professor Harmon."

"Deniro, Pinero, tomato, tomahto, let's call the whole thing off," the woman behind the desk sang tunefully. She was large and untidy, with huge horn-rimmed glasses and a lopsided grin. "Of course. Take a seat, if you can find one. So, any news? Can we assume foul play has been discovered?"

Melinda moved a pile of books to the floor and sat down.

"We are still at a preliminary stage of our investigation," she said a little primly. "You might be able to help answer some questions we have regarding projects Professor Harmon was working on at the time of her death."

"I'll do what I can. I'm not really in the English department. My area is Women's Studies, but I'm housed here until the college acknowledges Women's Studies as a legitimate independent discipline. Some in the department have been more welcoming than others. Geraldine was a good friend and supporter. I'll miss her…"

Melinda allowed a tactful pause while Betsy grabbed for a tissue and scrubbed at her nose.

"Do you know if anything was worrying her? Any conflict in the department that might have impacted her?"

Betsy thought for a moment. "Geraldine was an advocate for under-represented voices. I know it doesn't sound like a specialist in nineteenth-century literature would have much to say about systemic racism or me-too issues, but she was very empathetic. She could make connections between literature and real life. And she was very popular with students." She looked over her glasses at Melinda. "I guess what I'm leading up to say is that the leadership of the college and this department is quite conservative, and Geraldine was a voice for change. I know she was frustrated, but she avoided open conflict. Unlike yours truly!" Betsy gave a rueful smile.

"Do you know anything about a manuscript Professor Harmon was promoting that went missing?" Melinda heard Barry's voice in her ear chiding, "Open ended questions only!"

Betsy's gaze sharpened. "Yes! She'd befriended a young journalist. She was trying to get him here on a fellowship of some kind to work on a book, but that didn't develop. Then she told me he'd gone AWOL along with his manuscript. I think she felt responsible. I don't know why—but that was typical Geraldine."

Although Melinda probed a bit more, Betsy had revealed the extent of her knowledge. Melinda hurried back to wait outside Professor Hersch's door. Within a few minutes, that door opened and the professor ushered out a good-looking young man with a scowl on his face.

"Well, Mr. Johansen, if the course is proving too much for you, I suggest you audit it this year and try again next year when, no doubt, we will have filled the faculty vacancy. This late in the term, we can't possibly authorize a refund, no matter what the unfortunate circumstances." Professor Hersch turned to Melinda without waiting for the student to respond. "I just have a few minutes. Come in, come in."

Melinda felt an absurd urge to apologize to the young man for the professor's brusqueness, but he had already rushed away down the hall. She followed Hersch back into his office.

Ten minutes of open-ended questions elicited nothing but platitudes about how Professor Harmon was respected for her scholarship, well-regarded by colleagues and students alike, and would be sorely missed, so Melinda plunged in.

"What can you tell me about the journalist she wanted to come here?"

"Oh, that!" Hersch tossed back his leonine head of white hair and sighed. "Yes, yes, she had some idea about making this man a 'Writer in Residence.' I had to remind her that we're a Department of English Literature, not a journalism school!" The way he said the word "journalism" made his scorn clear. "Anyway, I offered to look over his manuscript, just as a professional favor, but I don't think she ever gave it to me. Personally, I think she'd been taken in. Some hack who couldn't get a visa playing on her sympathy. Maybe there never was a manuscript."

"Hmm. Just in case this has relevance to her death, could you nail down a timeline? Perhaps there are emails…?" Melinda noticed the absence of a computer on the professor's desk.

"Ask Anne. She handles all that." He gave a dismissive wave. "Now, I really must prepare for my seminar."

*What an awful man,* Melinda thought as she left the office, then switched gears to plan how to charm the frosty Ms. Summers. It turned out cooperation was easy to obtain. Whether the Senior Administrative Assistant was pleased to show off her facility with the computer or was eager to be part of a murder inquiry, Melinda couldn't tell, but after rapid click-clacks on the keys and earnest scrolling, a printer coughed into life to spew out pages. Melinda scanned the email thread. The exchange was initiated by Professor Harmon, introducing Michael Obrador, a journalist she had met at a conference, who was writing an exposé of government corruption and state-sponsored violence in Central America. Because of the sensitive content, Obrador needed a quiet, out-of-the-way place to complete the work in progress. Could the college offer him a temporary home? She suggested possible programs and sources of funds that might be used. After an "out-of-office" reply and a reminder from

Geraldine, the chair of the department responded in verbose sentences which boiled down to "No way." Being Professor Hersch, several paragraphs elaborated the theme. In the conclusion, Hersch made what he no doubt thought was a generous offer to "take a glance at the manuscript and see if he had thoughts on where it might be placed." Geraldine appealed her proposal's rejection in urgent terms. However, there was no further email response from Hersch.

"I don't see that Professor Harmon ever attached the manuscript to her emails," Melinda commented. "Do you know if she handed him a hard copy?"

"I remember some discussion afterward." Anne Summers waved a hand at the sheaf of papers in Melinda's hand. "It was summer. We weren't as busy as usual, and he asked me to see if Professor Harmon still wanted him to review the manuscript. She said, 'Yes. I'll bring it in and you can print out the first chapters.' She knew he didn't like to read online, so it would have to be hard copy." Ms. Summers' brows drew together in a frown. "But she never did bring it in. Strange…"

"You're quite sure she said she'd 'bring it in'? It wasn't on the computer she already had in her office?" Melinda probed.

"*Quite* sure." Ms. Summers was on the point of becoming defensive again, but then she relented. "I suppose I assumed the document was on a thumb drive she had at home. Anyway, term started and I thought no more about it. Nor did Professor Hersch, apparently."

\*\*\*\*

After an hour in the alley excavating the dumpster's contents, Fish and Melinda failed to find any discarded hypodermic syringes, disposable coffee cups, or anything else of possible relevance to Geraldine's death.

"Okay, let's go back to the ops center," the detective sergeant announced, to Melinda's relief. The odor was beginning to get to her. "Probably just as well we didn't find anything. The captain would have vetoed the cost of DNA analysis."

As they'd been searching, Melinda had filled Fish in on the information gleaned from neighbors and colleagues. She had taken his grunts, muffled by a surgical mask, as approval. In his car on the way back to the police department building, it was her turn to ask about his second interview with Diana Latour.

"Well, nothing new. She really doesn't like Thomas, but she has nothing concrete to link him to Geraldine's death."

Melinda guessed her boss had spent most of the interview trying to impress the attractive Ms. Latour with his intelligence and sophistication. Feeling new confidence in her own investigative skills, she risked a comment, "So, a waste of time, then."

"Not entirely." Fish's eyes were on the road but he was smiling. "Mr. Harmon has spent the days since his wife's death hiding away at home, avoiding phone calls and visitors. He didn't even notify Geraldine's parents of the death until the third day, and he's left it to them and Diana to make funeral arrangements."

"Totally distraught by his loss?" Melinda's question was cynical.

"Or up to something." Fish made it a statement. "When we executed the search warrant at the Harmon house, we were focused on finding Geraldine's laptop and phone. Did you notice if Thomas had his own computer?"

"Yes, he had a whole office set up in the back bedroom. He works from home. The warrant didn't stretch to his devices."

They continued the rest of the journey in silence, as Melinda and Barry's brains churned and whirred. What *was* Thomas Harmon up to?

****

After leaving Professor Hersch's office, Marco walked off his anger, striding through the campus, his thunderous expression chilling any approach from fellow students. He paid no attention to his surroundings, seeing only the old man's smug face as he shattered Marco's dreams of getting an education and having a future. He had to pass all his first-year classes to progress to a second year of college. If he failed Intro to English Lit and forfeited the tuition, as Hersch said he would, Marco would have to drop out. He had maxed out his student loans. The job at the Mission, part of his addiction recovery plan, paid minimum wage. Now, faced with losing his subsidized accommodation, the narrow financial margin that kept him afloat was disappearing. Hersch didn't care. No one did.

An hour later, at dusk, he found himself pounding the downtown streets. Every second building seemed to be a bar or brewpub. The urge to enter and order a drink was overwhelming. A tall IPA. No, a whiskey, more suitable for the wintry season. He could almost feel the warmth of the alcohol spreading down his throat and through his body. Outside one of the drinking establishments, he slowed to look in as a customer left. Then, his hand already outstretched to catch the open door before it closed, he heard the familiar words of his counselor in his head. *You know you can't stop at one.*

*And alcohol's just the gateway drug: before the night's over, you'll be down at the waterfront looking for something—anything—to get high, and promising God knows what in payment because you'll have spent all your money in the bar. You'll lose your job, too.*

This last thought caused him to check the time: just forty-five minutes until his shift at the shelter started. He could do this! He headed out of downtown, eyes on the sidewalk ahead of him, hands clenched into fists in his pockets. He should have gone to a meeting today instead of fighting this battle alone. Too late now. The Mission building stood ahead: his sanctuary. Once inside, the routine would take over and he'd be safe.

****

By 9:30 p.m., things had settled down, the meal staff had signed out, and most of the men were already stretched out on their cots and snoring. Satisfied that those remaining awake were chatting quietly or reading the dog-eared paperbacks and comics that comprised the Mission's library, Marco retreated to the employee lounge. He was glad Cindy was the overnight volunteer. Cindy knew all the procedures and needed no instructions. She wasn't overly chatty like some of the others, who were eager to explain in detail why they had volunteered at the shelter and expound on their brilliant ideas for solving the homeless crisis.

He flopped down on a sofa and opened his biology textbook. His problems swarmed over him again as he tried to concentrate. What was the point of studying if he was going to drop out? Then what if he *did* scrape through Intro to English Lit.? He couldn't afford to fail Biology.

"Problems?" Cindy's voice startled him out of his

circular thinking.

"What?" Marco wondered if he'd let out a sigh or if his facial expression had given him away.

"You haven't turned a page for ten minutes. Anything I can help with? I should warn you it's been twenty years since I was in college. We took notes on stone tablets in those days." Cindy was sitting on the other sofa with a paperback open on her knees. Her gaze at Marco was direct but friendly.

He put the textbook down and swung up to a seated position facing her. "It's not the class," he said. Before he could think about whether it was appropriate to confide in her, Marco let it all spill out: the housing problem, the money problem, the Professor Hersch problem, even the addiction problem. "I was doing okay until Professor Harmon died. It's like everything turned against me after that."

Cindy was silent, her eyes still on Marco's face.

"Do you remember Jesús, the guy who threw up?" she said eventually.

Puzzled, Marco replied, "Yes...?" He recalled the story Joan and Bill had shared about Jesús being on the run from some gang. "I haven't seen him around here for a while."

"He's safe. He found...sanctuary, got help. *Accepted* help."

*What did she mean?* He wondered how she knew about Jesús being in danger. But that wasn't her point.

"I have a spare room at my house. It's yours, if you want."

Marco looked at Cindy through narrowed eyes. There had to be a catch. What would she want in return?

"I can't afford much rent," he said. Did she want sex

with him? He'd never got that vibe from her. If anything, he'd assumed she was a lesbian.

"No rent, but there's a condition," Cindy replied.

*Uh oh.*

"Stop blaming fate or other people for your problems. Admit you are powerless—"

"The Twelve Steps. Alcoholics Anonymous," Marco interrupted.

"Yes. Do you go to meetings?"

Marco shrugged. "I did for a time. Not recently."

"Perhaps you should start again. Look, Marco, I like you, and I think you have potential. I want to help."

"But…?" Marco couldn't help the sullen note in his voice.

"No buts. Let's just say I'm trying to be a better person. I want to help," she repeated.

Marco took a deep breath. "Okay," he said. Perhaps it *would* be okay.

**\*\*\*\***

Cindy smiled as she watched Marco sleeping. A silvery line of drool crept from the corner of his half-open mouth. Without the tense frown of worry that had gripped his face earlier, he looked much younger, even angelic. She pondered how faces could transform, thinking of Jesús's smile and how it illuminated his face; of Joan and Bill, the energy and conviction that shone out of them in spite of wrinkled skin and gray hair. Before she'd met these three, especially Jesús, it wouldn't have occurred to her to offer to share her space with Marco. She would have lent a sympathetic ear, sure, maybe given some advice, but an inner reserve—her loner streak—would have prevented her getting more directly involved. She had her neatly ordered life, her modest business, the dog, rock climbing and backpacking, the mortgage-free Craftsman bungalow. She had friends she could call if she wanted company, but she treasured her independence. The weekly night shift at the Mission was perfect. It made her feel useful, but after she left in the morning, she didn't think about the men who slept there, or the stories that brought them to homelessness. She had told herself she was respecting their privacy by not asking intrusive questions, but she was beginning to realize that really she was protecting herself against involvement, against caring.

She considered asking Bill whether Marco could be included in the secret of where Jesus was hiding. It couldn't hurt to have another person in the group that now supported and protected the fugitive. The three of them, plus Father Odell, had formed a rota to deliver food and other necessities to Jesús in the Old School. However, they had progressed no further in developing a plan to remove the threat of the *Cofradia*. Perhaps Marco would have some fresh ideas.

Chapter 12

The rain was relentless, not coming down hard, just insidious and depressing. *Appropriate weather for a funeral,* thought Diana, as she shook out her umbrella and entered the funeral home.

If "funeral" was the word for the abbreviated service held in the building's crematorium. A tired-looking female pastor recited some non-denominational prayers, then invited the bereaved to share their thoughts about— consulting her notes—Geraldine. Thomas read a poem by Emily Dickinson, noting that she was his wife's favorite poet. He read well, but his face remained impassive and he failed to make eye contact with Mr. and Mrs. Riley or Diana, the only other mourners. Then Mr. Riley stepped forward to the podium. He could barely get a sentence out before he collapsed into sobbing and stumbled back to his seat, shaking his head. The pastor concluded with a eulogy long on platitudes about time being a healer, but short on specific references to the deceased. Recorded organ music masked the sound of the machinery that moved the coffin through the velvet curtains to the Great Beyond, and the congregants were dismissed with a blessing.

As Diana followed the Rileys out, she noticed another attendee standing at the back of the chapel: the young woman detective who had sat in on her first interview with Barry Fish. The detective, whose name she could not remember, smiled but did not insert herself into the group that then huddled under the portico. Thomas approached Maureen Riley, kissed her on the cheek, and pressed the book he had read from into her hands.

"Geraldine would have wanted you to have this," he said. He turned to shake Mr. Riley's hand before the grieving mother could summon a response, then strode off into the rain without acknowledging Diana.

"Well, really!" Mrs. Riley's face was flushed with anger. "Could he not have invited us back to the house for a cup of tea at least?" She looked at the little volume in her hands, her mouth trembling. "I just wanted to see where she lived, touch her things…"

Her husband put his arms around her and rested his cheek against her head. Diana, who had managed to control her emotions to this point, felt tears starting.

The Rileys would fly back to Boston the following day. Diana had invited them to dinner with her at a quiet little restaurant in town, but it was still too early to go there. She had done some research into local Catholic churches earlier in the day and now came up with a suggestion.

"St. Xavier's has a Saturday five o'clock mass. Would you like to go?"

The couple agreed that this was exactly what they needed to counteract the unsatisfactory funeral and Thomas's brusque retreat. They hurried through the rain to Diana's car for the short journey across town.

Although Diana was not religious, when she entered the interior of the candlelit Victorian church, with its dark wood pews and columns soaring into shadows, the faint smell of incense hovering in the air, she realized it was what she needed too.

The congregation consisted of no more than a dozen, mostly elderly and female. Diana sat in silence while the others stood, sat and kneeled, and voiced muffled responses to the priest's resonant, Irish-accented baritone. Peace crept over her, and she found she could at last think about Geraldine without lapsing into frustration and anger.

The priest concluded the service with a hearty "Peace be with you!" startling her out of her reverie. The congregants began to greet each other, and the priest moved forward, shaking hands and exchanging a few words with each member. After hugging the Rileys, Diana turned to greet the worshippers in the pew behind her. They had edged in after the service started, an elderly couple either side of a young, dark-haired man. Their son? Diana thought not: his coloring was different, Hispanic perhaps, while they were decidedly Anglo.

The priest had reached the Rileys. "Hello, I don't think I've seen you here before. Are you newcomers to town?"

"No, we're visiting—" Mr. Riley's face crumpled. He was unable to continue the explanation.

"Our daughter died. We're here for the funeral," Mrs. Riley completed, before she too started weeping. Diana put her arm around her, while the priest grasped her husband's hand in both of his.

"I am so very sorry. How can I help you?" His face and tone showed genuine concern.

"Could you—I know we're not parishioners—but could you say a mass for her?" Mrs. Riley asked.

"Of course. Tell me her name." From within the folds of his chasuble, the priest withdrew a tiny notebook with a pencil.

"Geraldine Harmon. We always called her Gerry."

Diana sensed a stir in the row behind, and turned in time to see the old couple exchange a meaningful look. After writing down the name, the priest moved across the aisle to greet other worshippers.

"Excuse me, I couldn't help overhearing." The old man in the pew behind leaned forward, keeping his voice low. "Did you say your daughter was called Gerry?"

"Yes," Mr. Riley confirmed. "Did you know her? She was a professor at the college."

"No-oo," the man admitted. "But we may have a connection in common." He glanced up at the young man next to him who had been watching the exchange with a puzzled frown.

Diana stared, realization dawning. She addressed the dark-haired man. "Are you Michael?"

Now all three stared back at her, their mouths falling open. Seconds passed before the man replied.

"*No. Michael está muerta.*"

Chapter 13

The alarm on Thomas's phone was set for 5:30 a.m.
He wanted to see if there was a response to his proposal.
The *Atlantic*, the *New Yorker*, the *Nation*—all had their
editorial offices on the East Coast, three hours ahead.
First, he would shower and dress, but breakfast and even
coffee could wait.

As Thomas soaped himself, he contemplated the
huge amount of work to do. His plan was to publish the
article as a teaser, then parlay it into a book deal. He had
to fact-check everything before revising the manuscript
to reflect his own writing style. This would mean
research trips to Central America. Other than a spring
break in Cancun when he was a student, and a week at a
Costa Rican ecolodge a couple of years ago—
Geraldine's idea—he had no knowledge of the region.
Thomas estimated at least a year before he'd be ready.
The sooner the house was on the market, the better. He'd
need a chunk of capital to fund the research, as well as a
move back east to Boston or New York, where the real
literary action was.

By six a.m. he was sitting at his computer. No e-mail
awaited him from an enthusiastic magazine editor
summoning him across the country for a meeting. No e-
mails for him at all. By force of habit, he logged into
Geraldine's account. Early in their marriage, they had
edited each other's writing and had exchanged

passwords and user IDs to facilitate access. The mutual editing practice fell quickly by the wayside, but Thomas had retained her passwords and user ID information, and liked to browse her e-mails from time to time. He hadn't told Geraldine what he was doing. She was so uptight about personal integrity and professional standards. In his own mind, he was just keeping up to date on developments in the academic world—nothing wrong in that. If he hadn't kept an eye on her inbox, he'd never have seen the manuscript to begin with, and what a loss that would have been to the publishing world. Yes, Geraldine *had* mentioned Michael, the young journalist she'd met at a conference, and how she was trying to get him some sponsorship, but he'd tuned it out as just another of her causes. Only when Thomas glimpsed the first pages of Michael's manuscript had he understood what a hot property his wife had discovered. The journalist had tried to dress the work as fiction with a few made-up names and fantastical locations, but it was clear to Thomas, a journalist himself, that power lay in telling the true story. He had downloaded the manuscript onto a thumb drive, and a good thing he had, because the next time he went snooping, both the manuscript and the e-mail chain between Geraldine and Michael had been deleted from her computer—completely deleted, from the trash folder as well.

This might explain why Geraldine had become so neurotic, staring into space for minutes at a time, flinching at the sound of his voice. She'd started taking her laptop with her everywhere, even sleeping with it next to the bed. He'd wondered if she'd found out about his intrusion into her online correspondence, but as she didn't change her passwords he concluded she must be fearful of something or someone else. When, after her death, he had used her e-mail address to reach out to Michael and had received no response, he suspected that Michael's "novel" had stirred up a hornet's nest and he had gone into hiding. All the more reason why he, as an experienced, independent, and objective voice, should handle this explosive material.

There was nothing new in Geraldine's inbox except a few impersonal announcements from list-servs; by now, all her friends and colleagues knew of her death. The need for sustenance, especially caffeine, occurred to Thomas. He was about to go downstairs when he heard a noise. His first thought was that Hannah had found a way in and was coming to force her sympathy on him again. He must keep her out of his office at all costs. But the figure that burst through the door was not Hannah. It was a big man in a ski mask, dressed in black and carrying a duffel bag.

"Give me that!" The man pointed at Thomas's laptop, still open to Geraldine's e-mail screen.

"No!" Thomas closed the laptop and held it to his chest, at the same time struggling to his feet.

The man towered over him. He plucked the computer out of Thomas's arms like a toy from a child, dropped it into the duffel, and gave a short laugh. "Now, your phone?"

Instinctively, Thomas glanced at his desk where the phone lay, face down. The man grabbed it, then with a sweep of his arm sent folders from their neat piles onto the floor. Papers floated out in a slow-motion snowstorm.

"No…" Thomas said again, this time more a moan than a protest. He tried to sidle toward the door, but the intruder pinned him against a file cabinet, hot, spicy-smelling breath in Thomas's face, an arm across his throat,

"Sit!"

Thomas sat. "Look, what do you want? My wallet's in the bedroom. Take that. I won't say anything. Just leave me the computer."

The man extracted some bungee cords from the bag and wound them around Thomas's body, immobilizing him before he could think to resist. Not that physical resistance would have occurred to him anyway—he had always relied on the power of words.

"Where is it?"

The man's breath was in Thomas's face again. Thomas could see dark eyes glistening through the holes in the mask. He shrank back as far as he could and stuttered, "In the bedroom—my wallet—take it. Please…"

The intruder ignored him, looking around the room and speaking now as if to himself, "Where is it?" When he looked back at Thomas, something cold and menacing in his eyes made his victim quake. He rummaged in the bag again. Thomas couldn't see what he withdrew.

"Please…" Thomas tried again, but was cut short by a stinging pain in his thigh. He looked down to see a hypodermic syringe in a black-gloved hand. "No! What are you doing?" He struggled against the cords and kicked out, losing a shoe in the process. The man had already stepped back out of reach and stood watching.

\*\*\*\*

After dropping the Rileys off at the airport—more tears as they said their farewells—Diana headed for the coffee shop where she was to meet Hannah and the others to plan the intervention that would shake Thomas loose from his isolation. She had spent half the night trying to connect the crumbs of information she had acquired about Geraldine's death to Thomas's possible role in it. The man at St. Xavier's was not Michael, the journalist Geraldine had tried to help, but someone who knew him. And he knew Michael was dead. The old couple had hustled him away before Diana could ask any more questions. She hoped she could find him again through the priest. In the meantime, a confrontation with Thomas might reveal the connections she sought.

Hannah was sitting alone, shredding a napkin with her long, purple-painted nails, an almond milk chai latte cooling in front of her.

"Where are the others?" Diana asked.

"Maisie had to take her husband to a cardiologist appointment. Gus and Penny begged off. They said they felt they didn't know Thomas well enough and didn't want to interfere." Hannah's chin tilted up at a defiant angle, challenging Diana to chicken out as well.

Diana smiled back. Although her motives were quite different from Hannah's—the poor woman seemed to be besotted with Thomas—she was determined not to miss out on a chance to get into Thomas's house, and perhaps under his skin. "Well, shall we go?"

"Don't you want anything?" asked Hannah with a jerk of her head toward the barista.

"No, I had coffee at home." *Black, no sugar*, Diana thought with a glance at the creamy confection on the table. Hannah gulped down half her drink, stood up, and reached for the cape-like garment thrown over the back of her chair. Diana pressed her lips together to suppress a small judgmental smile. Hannah didn't wear clothes so much as dress in costume. Today she appeared to be channeling her inner toreador: tight black velvet jeans, high-heeled boots, and a silky red blouse with plunging neckline and ruffles. The cape, now swirling around Hannah's shoulders, was black-and-white houndstooth lined in pink. As they left the coffee shop, Hannah presented a startling contrast to Diana, clothed in her trademark neutral tones in cashmere and tailored tweed.

They took separate cars to the Harmon residence. When Diana joined Hannah on the front porch, the other woman was jabbing repeatedly at the doorbell.

"See? He's not answering," Hannah said.

Diana stepped back from the porch and surveyed the windows at the front of the house. A low winter sun reflected off the glass, revealing nothing of the interior. "Try calling him," she suggested.

Hannah had Thomas's number on speed-dial—of course she did. Diana leaned toward the front door to see if she could pick up the sound of the phone ringing inside. Nothing. "Let's try around the back."

As they passed along the side of the garage, Diana stopped to peer through a window. Thomas's ten-year-old, cherry-red BMW was inside. At the back of the house, Hannah repeated her attack on the doorbell while Diana moved along to the kitchen window. Inside, the countertops were clear, except for coffeemaking paraphernalia laid out in a row like surgeon's tools. The sink was empty of dishes.

Hannah was calling out, "Tommy!" in rising tones of panic. Before the neighbors could come running to see what the commotion was about, Diana laid a hand on Hannah's sleeve. "Wait a minute." She crossed the patio to a row of pots containing the remnants of last season's herbs. She moved the one on the far left and extracted a key from underneath.

Hannah's mouth dropped open. "Why didn't you say you knew where the key was?"

Diana ignored her, fitted the key in the lock, and opened the back door. Miffed, Hannah pushed past, still calling out Thomas's name. Diana followed, checking each of the downstairs rooms as she passed through. She touched the electric kettle in the kitchen: cold. She could make out paler stripes left by a vacuum cleaner on the living room rug. All surfaces were dust-free. The house had a sterile, empty feel.

When Diana climbed the stairs, she found Hannah hovering outside a closed door. She was surprised to feel a glimmer of sympathy for the other woman. Hannah was selfish and shallow, but her concern for Thomas was genuine. "I don't think he's here," Diana said.

"What if he's…" Hannah nodded toward the door, her voice dropping to a dramatic whisper "…harmed himself?" Before Diana could answer, Hannah threw open the door to reveal the master bedroom. The king-size bed was neatly made, there were no discarded clothes strewn over chairs or drawers left half out. The only detail that distinguished the bedroom from a medium-priced hotel room was a couple of books on the nightstand. Diana hesitated at the door, feeling squeamish about penetrating further, but Hannah had no such scruples. She charged across to the *en suite* bathroom and clattered around out of sight for a minute.

"Nope, you're right. He's gone." Hannah sounded angry now. She had been prepared to rescue Thomas from the brink of despair, to console and comfort him, perhaps dreaming she might, in time, divert him from his loss into a new relationship. The pristine state of the empty house indicated Thomas was doing just fine on his own.

Meanwhile Diana was thinking of Geraldine. There was no hint she had ever lived here. Thomas must have worked hard to remove all traces of his dead wife. If the books on the nightstand had been hers, they would be frilled with multi-colored sticky notes and a pair of reading glasses would be perched on top. Diana remembered perfume bottles and photos in frames on the dresser. One of those photos was of the two of them from Oxford days. The thought made Diana's throat close up with grief.

"Let's just check the other rooms," she suggested, not willing to give up hope that some echo of her friend's existence might persist. Or some clue to her death. The other bedroom at the front of the house was even more barren, a single bed with a bare mattress and packing boxes stacked against the wall. There was one more closed door at the other end of the landing. Diana opened it and took a step forward before she was stopped short by the contrast with the rest of the house. This room—an office—was in disarray: papers scattered on the floor, books swept off shelves. A pencil jar had rolled off the desk and shattered. Diana stared around taking in all the signs of a hasty and violent search.

Hannah came up behind her. "What the hell?"

Diana turned and held Hannah's upper arms. "No, don't come in. We mustn't touch anything." Hannah started to protest. Diana spoke over her. "We've got to call the police. I think Thomas has been kidnapped."

Beneath the desk, on its side, was one brown leather loafer, the style Thomas wore.

Chapter 14

Barry Fish asked Diana to describe the search of the Harmon residence, while Melinda Deniro interviewed Hannah sitting in the latter's parked car. The forensic team called in from the county sheriff's department were at work upstairs, so they wouldn't be able to go inside. Fish was keen to separate the witnesses. He guessed he'd get more information out of Diana, so delegated his junior to deal with Hannah's histrionics.

Diana led him around the side of the house, pausing to demonstrate how she had peered inside the garage and seen Thomas's car. When they reached the patio, she dug in her pocket for the backdoor key.

"Geraldine showed me where she hid this months ago. I can't remember why exactly." Diana showed him the plant pot under which the key had been left. "Should I replace it?"

"No, I'll take it," Fish replied, offering an open evidence bag. Diana dropped in the key, and the detective sealed it and placed it in his pocket. "Just describe exactly what you did and your impressions."

Diana took a deep breath and closed her eyes, taking herself back to when she and Hannah had stood together in this spot about an hour ago. Then she began describing in detail her progress through the house: the sparkling clean kitchen with the coffee grinder, coffee press, cup and spoon lined up precisely on the countertop; the living room, dusted and vacuumed, surfaces clear of the ornaments and personal items she remembered. "The books were all still on the shelves—at least, as far as I can remember—but everything else had been put away. No magazines. Even the drinks tray was gone."

"You were familiar with the house, then?"

"Oh, yes. I've been here several times when Geraldine was..." Diana turned away, reluctant to let Fish, pleasant though he was, witness her eyes welling up. She continued to explain how she had followed Hannah upstairs, and that she had noticed the same almost anal tidiness in the bedrooms. "I didn't go into the bathroom—Hannah did—but I expect it was the same."

"You say there were packing boxes in the spare bedroom? Do you think Mr. Harmon was planning to move?"

"I hadn't thought of that, but yes, it's like the house has been prepared for sale."

Just then, the forensic team—a photographer and two crime scene technicians—filed out the back door. Barry thanked Diana and asked her to get in touch if she thought of anything else. She left, and he turned to the senior CS tech.

The officer stripped off his paper protective gear as he spoke. "No fingerprints except the homeowner's. We've taken carpet samples, but there's no point in testing until you find a suspect. Professional lock-picking job on the front door, I'd say, unless it was left unlocked. Looks like the victim was immobilized and dragged down the stairs: slight scuff marks. I think they went out the same way they came in, but there's no trace outside. They must have kept to the paved path."

"You say 'they'? More than one attacker?" Fish

asked.

The tech blew air out through pursed lips. "Don't know. How big's the victim? One guy could have done it."

Fish let the team go, following them around to the front of the house. He looked for Melinda to tell her to start a canvas of the neighbors, but he couldn't find her. Diana and Hannah had already left in their own cars, and the police vehicle stood empty.

****

Melinda had a difficult job detaching herself from Hannah. Mascara streaks augmenting her appearance, Hannah felt a need to go over her entire history with Thomas Harmon.

"...And I was the first here to offer my sympathy and support after his wife died," she concluded. "That was when I met you, only you were in uniform then."

"Right. So, is there anything else you can tell me about this morning? Anything unusual you noticed?" Melinda had asked this already, but Hannah's response had derailed into reminiscence. This time she just shook her head, and Melinda took the opportunity to give her one of her newly printed business cards: *Detective Melinda Deniro*. "If you remember anything—I mean, about this morning—give me a call."

She got out of the car and walked back to the police car. She waited until Hannah drove off before heading to Ellie Posner's house. Ellie was likely to be a more useful witness.

After declining an offer of coffee and cookies—"I took them out of the oven twenty minutes ago. They're still warm"—Melinda asked if Mrs. Posner had noticed any unusual activity in the street.

"You mean the man in the parked car? No, he's not been back. At least, I haven't seen him when I go out to fetch my paper." Ellie considered, her head tipped to one side. "There was a car earlier. I heard a car door slam twice. It was still dark and I was in bed. My bedroom's at the front, and I always leave a window cracked open, even in winter. It's healthier to sleep in a cool room, you know."

Melinda began to regret refusing the cookies as she listened to Mrs. Posner ramble. She knew the elderly woman would get to the point in the end, and her observations would be accurate.

"It's so inconsiderate to slam doors at that hour of the morning. I was already awake—I wake up early these days—but even so. I thought of going to the window to see who it was, but I didn't bother. I just turned over and told Alexa to play NPR. That's how I know it was 6:30. They always do a recap of the top stories at half past the hour."

"And you're sure you heard the car door slam twice?" Melinda asked.

Ellie widened her eyes in surprise at the question. "Of course! Didn't I say so? Once would be bad enough, but twice!"

Melinda smiled. She would interview the other neighbors as a routine matter, but she was fairly sure they would add nothing to Ellie's recall.

"Do take some of these cookies back with you," her star witness urged. "Otherwise, I'll eat them all myself. Not good for my girlish figure!" She giggled.

\*\*\*\*

When Aubrey left the house at 9:30, her car wouldn't start. She turned the key multiple times, the volume and intensity of her curses increasing with each savage twist. Giving up, she went back into the house for her mother's car keys.

"Mom!" she yelled, when she didn't find the keys or Hannah's purse on the kitchen counter where they usually lived. The house remained silent. What could be so important as to take her mother—and her car!—out before 9:30 a.m.? Aubrey was forced to call an Uber, seething with resentment at having to spend her own hard-earned cash.

Her bad mood lasted through her morning classes, dissipating only as she emerged from the lecture hall at noon. She decided to drop by the cafeteria to see if Marco was there. He wasn't, but she sat down with two samosas and a vitamin water anyway, congratulating herself on making healthy food choices. Marco hadn't been around much lately. Maybe he was in the library with the nerds studying for the looming end-of-term exams. She wouldn't search for him there. That place gave her the creeps—rows of heads bent over books, no sound except pages turning. Her study habits were more spontaneous, like the night before a big test, and she preferred an energizing buzz of activity around her.

Aubrey's shift at the Mermaid's Closet started at 2 p.m. The store was the other side of town but she rejected the idea of calling another Uber. She stood at the bus stop for five minutes, puzzling over the route map and timetable affixed to the shelter. Then she remembered she'd never picked up her free student bus pass anyway, so she gave up. Other students walked from campus to downtown all the time, so how hard could it be? It was mostly downhill, and not raining at the moment. Her mood brightened further at the prospect of a pleasant afternoon—paid!—browsing the merchandise at her place of employment.

When she was in sight of the store, Aubrey consulted her phone to see what time it was. She would be more than a half hour early. Would Mr. Karapoulas be pleased because he could make a quick getaway to whatever occupied his afternoons? Or maybe he'd be irritated at her unannounced change of schedule? And would she be paid for the extra work time? Unsure of the protocols covering the situation, she paused and considered backtracking, but it had started raining again, and there were no other shops around to duck into. She pulled up her hoodie and started forward, noticing for the first time a man standing twenty feet ahead on the sidewalk. He must have stepped out of an alley between the buildings. The man, middle-aged, white and unremarkable in appearance, was gazing around as if lost, rain forming dark splotches on his pale blue dress shirt. *What an idiot to leave home without a coat in December*, Aubrey thought. *Perhaps he's stoned*. At that moment, his head turned toward her, and she recognized him.

"Mr. Harmon!" she called. On principle, she avoided her mother's friends, and refused to make note of their names, but Thomas Harmon was married to her English professor, the same professor whose dead body she had discovered less than two weeks before, and Hannah had gone on and on about "poor Tommy" ever since, so she couldn't help acknowledging him.

"Hi, I'm Aubrey, Hannah's daughter?" She said as she approached. He looked at her without recognition. His hair was plastered to his head, and raindrops fell off his nose. Glancing down, she was taken aback to see he was only wearing one shoe. "Hey, what happened to your shoe?"

Thomas looked down as if noticing the absence of footwear for the first time. Still, he said nothing.

"Look, I work at that store," Aubrey pointed to the Mermaid's Closet. "You want to come in out of the rain?"

At last he responded, mumbling his thanks. He followed her through the shop door, his unshod foot making squelching sounds.

Mr. Karapoulas looked up, smiling when he saw Aubrey, then drawing his brows together at the sight of the bedraggled figure accompanying her.

"Mr. K, this is Thomas Harmon. He's a friend of my mom's." Aubrey dropped her voice to a stage whisper. "He's lost a shoe. I think he's…" She tilted her head to the side and squinted her eyes, trying to convey with subtlety that Thomas might not be in full possession of his faculties.

"Come and sit down, sir." As she had hoped, Mr. K assessed the situation and took charge. "Aubrey, go get one of those stadium blankets," he said, indicating a display stand.

"But…" Aubrey knew the throws bedecked with logos of professional and college sports teams were the most expensive item in the store. *Well, it's his store.* She shrugged, selected one with her favorite blue and green colors, and stripped off the plastic wrapping. Mr. Karapoulas sat Thomas down on the stool behind the counter and draped the cover around his shoulders.

"Now, can you tell me what happened?"

Thomas slowly focused on Mr. Karapoulas's face. "I was attacked."

"Then we should call the police," Mr. K said, looking to the shop window now obscured by streaks of rain. "They might still be out there."

"No!" Thomas's reply was sharp. "No police. I mean, I wasn't attacked here. It was earlier." His voice faded again. "I don't feel well. I just want to go home."

"Aubrey, go and make some tea for Mr. Harmon." Mr. K turned back to Thomas. "An ambulance, then. It might be concussion. You should get checked out."

Aubrey left them to it, Mr. K urging professional assistance and Thomas resisting, while she went into the storeroom at the back of the shop where an electric kettle and fixings for tea and coffee were kept. Waiting for the water to boil, she thought about calling Hannah. Her mom would be down here in a flash to smother Thomas with TLC, thrusting her chest out and batting her lashes. No, Aubrey would not call her. The Mermaid's Closet was *her* place, and Mr. K was *her* boss. More than a boss, really, although not quite a friend. He was an adult—perhaps the only one—who treated her with respect, who trusted and relied on her. She was not going to endanger that by exposing him to the spectacle of her mother, the drama queen.

She made a mug of tea, adding two sugars. Thomas Harmon didn't look like the kind who took sugar in his tea, but she had read somewhere—maybe in one of those boring English novels his professor-wife had made them read—that hot sweet liquids were good for people in shock. She carried the tea through to the store and handed it to Thomas. After a few sips, his color improved and he revived to the point of asking to borrow a phone to call a cab.

"No, no, let me drive you home, sir. It's no trouble,"

Mr. Karapoulas insisted, then turned to Aubrey. "That is, if you don't mind being left on your own, my dear? I think whatever happened to Mr. Harmon wasn't in this neighborhood, but you can always call me if you feel the slightest bit nervous."

"I'll be fine; don't worry about me," Aubrey replied. The doorbell jangled to announce the arrival of a customer, and to prove her competence she moved out from behind the counter to greet her. "Can I help you find something?"

When Mr. K and Thomas had gone and the customer had been served, Aubrey cleared away the tea mug and wiped down the counter. She wandered around the store straightening displays. Between customers, she imagined telling Marco about the coincidence of finding Mr. Harmon wandering around in a daze only days after they had found his wife dead. Weird. But maybe destined in a cosmic kind of way: the circle that brings people together? She spent a lot of time in imaginary conversation with Marco, especially during slow afternoons at work.

She picked up one of the mood pendants on sale for $9.99 and read the instructions: "Place against skin next to heart. Stone changes color to tell fate." She put eight dollars in the cash register, taking advantage of the 20% employee discount, and stripped away the packaging. She drew the cord over her head and pushed the pendant under her T-shirt until it rested between her breasts. While it warmed, she read over the color codes explained on the enclosed card. Bright green denoted "romance," but a darker green signified "mixed emotions," whatever that meant. Mid-blue indicated "calm and relaxed," while dark blue stood for "passion" and purple meant "very happy." Hmm, she would have associated purple with passion, rather than dark blue, but she guessed the two emotions might be interchangeable. She'd settle for an egg-yolk-yellow-verging-on-mustard: "lovable."

She fished out the pendant, and went over to the window to examine it in daylight. The oval stone shaded from blue to green, some spots darker than others. Not lovable then, but otherwise hard to read. Mr. K would be back soon to close; she'd ask his opinion. Perhaps she would confide to him about Marco, not that there was much to confide, she admitted to herself with a sigh.

She texted Hannah: "need ride at 6 pick me up corner maple street." At least she could keep her mother well away from Mr. K and the Mermaid's Closet.

Chapter 15

Cindy had arranged to meet Bill and Joan at the Bluebird at four o'clock, before the brewpub started filling up. With full pint glass in one hand and Josie's leash in the other, she made her way to the table they had chosen in the shadow of the huge stainless steel vats in which the beer was brewed.

The purpose of the meeting was to discuss next steps. Jesús couldn't hide out in the Old School for ever. Father Odell had felt compelled to inform his religious superiors of the fugitive's presence, and the more people who knew about him the less safe he was. But before they brainstormed alternatives, Bill and Joan told Cindy about their encounter at Saturday evening mass at St. Xavier's.

"We never thought that Gerry could be a woman," Bill concluded. "But is this Geraldine Harmon the person Michael entrusted his manuscript to? That would be a big coincidence."

"Well, here's another coincidence. You know Marco, the night manager at the Mission?" The couple nodded. "*He's* the person who found Geraldine Harmon's body. The police interviewed him. I think they're treating the case as a suspicious death."

"Really? I did some research and I couldn't find anything in the media except a statement from the college that her death was 'sudden and unexpected' and 'she will be greatly missed,' blah, blah," Joan said. "I don't see how an English professor who specializes in nineteenth century literature is involved with the *Cofradia*."

"Okay, but Michael mentioned this town to Jesús, as well as the name 'Gerry,' so there is a connection," Cindy replied. Then she remembered something else. "Marco told me someone came looking for Jesús at the Mission—a big man with a Hispanic accent. He offered Marco money for information."

Joan and Bill looked at each other in dismay.

"*Cofradia*. They're here," said Bill in a hushed voice. "What did Marco tell him?"

"Nothing. I think we should bring Marco in on this. He could be helpful. Anyway, he's moving into my house in a few days, and I don't want to be tiptoeing around him with secrets." Cindy saw Joan's smirk and added, "No, he's just a lodger. I'm letting him stay in my spare room."

"Marco's a good person," Bill agreed. "But this just confirms it; we have to do something. Jesús is in grave danger."

"How about we go to the police investigating Geraldine Harmon's death and tell them about the *Cofradia* connection?"

"No!" Bill and Joan said in unison. Their mistrust of law enforcement, based on decades of civil and not-so-civil protest, was entrenched. The three sat, staring into their beer, while Josie snoozed under the table.

Joan broke the silence. "When I was trying to find out more about Professor Harmon, I discovered her husband is a journalist, like Michael. Maybe we could take the story to him, and accomplish what Michael wanted: exposing the *Cofradia*'s activities. No one here cares what happens in Central America, but if the U.S. media link the *Cofradia* to the professor's death, the publicity might scare them off."

"That's a good idea, my love." Bill smiled for the first time that evening. "Perhaps Marco's the right person to approach Harmon, as he knew his wife. The poor man must be shattered by his loss. Playing a role in bringing this evil to light could help him move forward." Bill drained his glass. "Now we have a plan, how about another to celebrate?"

\*\*\*\*

In the Ops Center, Barry Fish was teetering again on the back legs of his chair while Melinda Deniro brewed yet another pot of coffee. She arranged the cookies Ellie Posner had insisted she take on a paper plate and placed them on the worktable. Then the two detectives sat, sipped and chewed, staring at the whiteboard now crammed with circled nuggets of information, each joined by lines to other circles or names. The entire board was punctuated with question marks.

Fish frowned, reluctant to relinquish his theory that Thomas Harmon was behind his wife's death but unable to come up with another possibility. "What connects the disappearance of Thomas to the death of Geraldine, other than the fact that they're married?"

Melinda paused before responding to see if her boss's question was rhetorical. "Um, I was thinking…"

"Good!" Fish interrupted with more sarcasm than intended, frustration getting the better of his usual laid-back demeanor.

"In both cases, their computers and phones were taken, suggesting the perpetrator was looking for information," Melinda continued in a rush, smarting from his caustic comment. She knew she should have more confidence in herself.

Fish turned a surprised gaze toward her. "That's it! You've got it! The deaths—well, we don't know Thomas is dead—are incidental. The answers are on the devices." He looked back at the board, missing Melinda's rapid flush of pleasure. "That manuscript Diana told us about—the one Geraldine never showed to her boss— could that be the motive? What do we know about it?"

"A journalist called Michael gave it to Professor Harmon at a conference in Arizona in April. She tried to get him a job at the college but was unsuccessful. Diana told us Geraldine was worried about something. Perhaps it's all connected."

"I need to talk to Diana again," Barry said, eyes gleaming. "And I'll work on getting Thomas's phone and email records. That might give us a lead." Melinda smiled to herself. Barry Fish might be an experienced detective, but he was as transparent as a teenager when it came to an attractive female witness.

Barry's phone rang. "Fish here…yes…what?… okay, we're on our way." He stood and headed for the door. "Grab your coat. That was the patrol officer stationed at the Harmon residence. Thomas Harmon's just turned up!"

****

Diana paced the patio, smoking with jerky movements that betrayed her nervous state. She had used up her weekly allowance of cigarettes in a single day, and another cup of coffee would only agitate her further. She needed something to calm her down and allow whatever buried anxiety nagging at her to surface.

Returning inside, she opened the refrigerator door to survey the contents. Yesterday's leftover kimchi would not do. She didn't even like kimchi, but had read extensive studies on its healthy effect on gut bacteria. Perhaps the no-fat Greek yogurt with some honey stirred in would answer her need for something comforting and creamy. Then she remembered the ice cream. When she had moved into Geraldine's sabbatical-traveling colleague's house, the refrigerator had been emptied and sparkling clean, but the absent and absent-minded professor had forgotten the freezer compartment. Nestled at the back surrounded by frost-obscured packages of mystery meat was an unopened pint of her favorite—cheesecake with caramel and chocolate.

*Never eat standing up* was one of Diana's unbreakable rules. Whether eating alone or with company, she always laid out a table setting with a clean napkin folded on the left and a water glass to the right. She stood now in front of the cupboard where glass compote dishes of the appropriate size for dessert were stored. *Aw, to hell with it!* Grabbing a spoon, she headed for the couch, and stretched out with the carboard tub of ice cream balanced on her belly. *At least I'm not standing up.* The chill penetrating through her clothes was not unpleasant. She stripped off the band that sealed the lid, opened it, and dug a spoonful out. As the sweet smoothness permeated her mouth, she breathed in deeply.

Several spoonfuls later, she moved the tub to the floor and closed her eyes. She let images from the day float through her mind—Hannah's extravagant costume, the backdoor key under the flowerpot, the sterile feel of the Harmon house's interior... That was it! What was bothering her was not something she had seen, but something missing. An absence that had lodged in her subconscious like a thorn. This was different than grief for her friend. Of course, she had felt Geraldine's absence in every room, but this feeling of loss was more specific.

The room darkened while she lay sprawled, breathing slowly and letting memories float up. She walked through Geraldine's house in her mind. When she entered the bedroom, the sight of the bare dresser top assaulted her. She remembered the framed photo that had stood there when Geraldine had taken her upstairs a few weeks ago to look at a new outfit she had purchased. The picture showed the women in an Oxford college quadrangle, squinting against the sun. The contrast between the two figures was striking: Geraldine's elfin face framed in a bush of red-gold hair, her short stature swamped by an academic gown. Diana's dark hair was pulled tightly back into a ponytail, she wore heavy-framed glasses, was a head taller…and fat. Diana had picked up the photograph. "Oh my God, I look awful in this! Why on earth do you have it on show?"

Geraldine had come up beside her and taken it out of her hands. "No, you were beautiful—a butterfly in its chrysalis, just about to emerge."

That was true. Back in Oxford, twenty-five years ago, Geraldine had made it true. At that moment in the college quad, Diana's life changed, and she began the journey away from an unhappy childhood, loneliness and lack of confidence, from frumpy, overlarge clothes and hiding in the library, to dancing, theatre and jumping into the Isis from Christ Church Meadows at dawn with a crowd of fellow undergraduates.

Diana sat up and swung her feet to the floor. She must have that photograph. It was probably packed away in those boxes she had seen in the spare room. She must retrieve it before it was disposed of. The urgency of her thought drove her to standing. Then she remembered the Harmon house was a crime scene. There was probably a policeman posted on guard, and even if not, she had given the key to Detective Fish. She had no means of entry.

Diana was angry now, her rage directed at Thomas Harmon. From the first time she met him, he had attempted to undermine her relationship with Geraldine. Jealousy perhaps, but the reason for his sarcasm and aloofness might also lie in the knowledge that he would never be equal to his wife in career or character. Diana of all people could recognize the scars that an unloved child brought to adulthood. Unlike her, Thomas had never found the internal resources to overcome self-doubt, and so had created a brittle veneer to protect himself from others' judgment. Diana should feel sorry for him. She didn't. She didn't care if he never reappeared except that, for the moment, he held hostage the thing she wanted.

Nevertheless, she would find a way into his house. Her friendship with Geraldine would not be erased.

****

"Why in God's name do I have to pick you up on a street corner after dark in a sketchy part of town? Why couldn't I come to the store?"

Aubrey was relieved of the burden of answering Hannah because her mother launched at once into a description of her adventure: the planned intervention to save "poor Tommy," the discovery that he had been "kidnapped—perhaps killed!" and her interview—"interrogation!"—by the police. "I am just out of my head with worry!" Hannah concluded as they pulled into the driveway.

Aubrey unbuckled and started to climb out of the car. "Well, you can stop worrying now. He turned up outside the Mermaid's Closet, and my boss gave him a ride home a couple of hours ago," she tossed over her shoulder. Hannah's shriek could have shattered crystal. She pounded after her daughter through the front door and up the stairs.

"Why didn't you text me? What was he doing there? Is he all right?" Her questions were cut off by Aubrey's bedroom door slamming closed. Aubrey listened to her mother's retreating footsteps. She could make out the sound of the refrigerator door opening in the kitchen and imagined Hannah reaching in for the chardonnay. *She probably consumed half the bottle before coming to pick me up,* Aubrey thought. *She'll finish the bottle and then decide to drive over to Thomas's house. Silly bitch.*

Chapter 16

The patrol officer got out of his car as Barry and Melinda drew up.

"Harmon's inside. He was dropped off by, er…" The officer pulled out his notebook and read out loud, "Iannos Karapoulas, an accountant. He said Harmon was wandering around down by the waterfront, no coat or shoes, and so he gave him a ride home. Said he'd never met him before. I have Karapoulas' contact information. Seemed like a straight-up guy, so I let him go."

"Okay. No point in you hanging around either. We'll go in and talk to Harmon."

The detectives waited a full minute after ringing the doorbell before Thomas called from inside. "Who is it? I can't speak to anyone right now. Come back tomorrow."

"It's Detectives Fish and Deniro, Mr. Harmon, and we need to speak to you *now*."

The door opened a few inches, enough to reveal Thomas Harmon in pajamas and a bathrobe.

"I'm exhausted. Can't this wait until tomorrow?"

Fish took a step forward, forcing Thomas to retreat.

"No, it can't wait. You do realize that we've been searching for you since this morning when you were reported missing, probably kidnapped? We need to know what happened. Let us inside."

"What do you mean 'reported missing'? Who

reported? One of the neighbors? They should mind their own business," Thomas said in a peevish voice, but realizing that Fish was not backing away, he opened the door wider and led them into the living room. He did not invite his visitors to sit. He stood fiddling with the sash of his robe, self-conscious to be found in his nightclothes at 6:30 p.m.

"Where's your computer, Mr. Harmon? And your phone?" Fish's tone was pleasant, but his eyes were steely. Thomas's jaw dropped for a second, but he recovered.

"Look, I was robbed early this morning. He surprised me in my study, probably didn't expect me to be up. He grabbed what he could and ran, I suppose. The computer, my phone… I haven't checked what else is missing yet."

"What did the burglar look like?"

"I couldn't tell you. He wore a ski mask. It was only a matter of seconds." Melinda noted Thomas's gaze shifting around the room, indicating that he was lying or not telling the whole truth. Fish let the silence hang, an invitation to an uncomfortable witness to start embroidering his story, but Thomas was smarter than that.

"So what happened to you between the intruder surprising you in your study and you being found wandering around in the rain this afternoon miles from here?" Fish sat down on the sofa, as if settling in for a long session. Melinda followed suit. Thomas remained standing, pulling the sash of his robe tighter.

"I…I'm not sure. I think he drugged me or something. I passed out. I came to in an abandoned building. I felt woozy, didn't know where I was. In fact,

I still feel unwell, so if you—" Thomas made a move toward the front door.

"How big was this burglar? Did he have an accent? Besides the ski mask, how was he dressed? Burglary and kidnapping are serious felonies, Mr. Harmon. Our investigation can't wait." Now Fish's voice was steel too.

"I can't help you. As I say, it was all over so very fast—"

"No, I think you *can* help us, not just about this *burglary*,"—the emphasis Fish placed on the word implied scorn—"but also your wife's death. We suspect they're connected."

Harmon's mouth opened, and he struggled to speak for a moment. "My wife? What do you mean? It was her heart. How is that connected to…" His voice trailed off.

Melinda thought Harmon's shock and confusion were genuine, and she felt some sympathy. "But, Mr. Harmon, you've seen the autopsy—"

Fish cut her off. "Who told you she died of a heart attack?"

"I think it was Professor Hersch. Yes, when he called that morning he said it was her heart. I never thought…" Again, Harmon's eye wandered over the room, as if looking for answers.

At that moment, Melinda realized Fish hadn't shared the autopsy findings with Thomas. It was standard protocol to share the report with the next-of-kin. Usually, the family pestered the police for cause of death, but here Thomas thought he already knew it, thanks to the officious head of the college's English Department. Fish had been so convinced Thomas played a role in killing Geraldine that he'd withheld information to which the husband was entitled. Melinda's previous unquestioned acceptance of Fish's competence cracked open. She watched him as he thought out his next question.

"Why were you so insistent on getting your wife's phone from the Medical Examiner? That was the only thing you asked about when you identified the body." Barry still hung onto his suspicions.

To both detectives' surprise, Thomas blinked back tears.

"I'd texted her that morning. I was angry with her. I didn't want anyone to see that the last thing I said to her was…unpleasant."

Melinda made a quick reassessment of Thomas's character. Maybe the coldness he had shown on her previous visits indicated the suppression of emotion, "denial" in the Kübler-Ross stages of grief. He would never win a Mr. Congeniality contest, yet he might still have human qualities.

She decided to take over the questioning. Melinda was surprised at Fish. He had distorted the course of the investigation because of a preconceived idea about Thomas's guilt. Perhaps he had also been swayed by the elegant Diana Latour's apparent distrust of her friend's husband. Melinda might be new to detection, but she understood enough to keep personal feelings out of it.

"So tell us what happened at home on the morning of Geraldine's death." Her voice indicated concern and compassion. Fish wisely let her continue.

Thomas exhaled a long breath and took a seat opposite the detectives.

"We had a row at breakfast."

"What about?"

"She accused me of snooping, of accessing her emails, 'infringing her privacy.' " Thomas's self-righteousness colored his confession. He might feel relief at telling the truth at last, but it would be *his* truth.

"And had you been accessing her computer?" Melinda persisted gently.

"Well, yes. In the past, we'd had no secrets from each other. I was always interested to see what she was working on. I knew she didn't much care for it, but I didn't think she would find out."

"The row. What happened?"

"She was furious, out of control. I put my hands on her shoulders to restrain her. She twisted away. I didn't mean to hurt her, but she was such a little thing—" Thomas's voice broke. This time, Melinda was not so convinced his emotion was genuine. The bruising was on Geraldine's neck, not her shoulders. However, the bruising had not contributed to her death, and even if shaded in his favor, Thomas's story was consistent with the facts they knew.

"Then you texted her?" Melinda prompted.

"Yes. She stormed out. I waited twenty minutes, thinking she would have calmed down by the time she got to her office. Then I sent her a message." Thomas chewed his lip, hesitating over how much to say, Melinda thought. "I told her she was hysterical, overreacting, and anyway the novel was crap and she'd make a fool of herself for promoting it."

Barry Fish straightened in his seat. "What novel?"

Melinda cursed internally. She thought Thomas was beginning to trust her, but Barry's accusatory tone might shut him down.

"Just some manuscript she'd fallen in love with. Or

maybe she'd fallen in love with the writer. She certainly seemed more interested in him than me." He gave a bitter laugh, then turned earnest. "I see how that sounds, but I didn't harm Geraldine. We might not have been in the first flush of love, but we got along…usually."

Melinda took over again. "What was the novel about, Mr. Harmon?"

"Oh, I'm not really sure, didn't read enough of it. I assume you have her computer. You can look for it yourself—and the emails she sent to the author." He was being evasive again.

"That's the point, Mr. Harmon. Her computer—and her phone—were missing from her office when the body was found. We assume they were taken by the person who caused her death. Now *your* computer and phone have gone missing after you were attacked in a similar fashion. So you see how important it is that you are absolutely honest with us. Your life might be in danger."

Thomas seemed to be digesting this. He sat very still, his eyes flicking to Barry and back to Melinda. Harmon was an unlikeable character, but he was not stupid. Melinda could almost see the wheels turning in his brain. She waited, hoping Fish would not disrupt the silence with another hostile question.

"Look, I'm just theorizing here, but say the novel isn't really a novel, say it's an exposé of some sort, I mean, based on actual facts—crimes, say—then I can see why someone would want to steal Geraldine's laptop to protect themselves from discovery. But the thing is…" Thomas looked down a moment before refocusing on Melinda. "I happen to know she had deleted the manuscript from her computer a couple of weeks before she died. So that's probably why they came after mine."

"Because you had made a copy of the manuscript for yourself," Melinda breathed the words out.

Thomas nodded, then smiled—a tight-lipped smirk. "So now they have what they want, I don't think they'll bother me again." He stood, indicating it was time for the detectives to leave.

Barry Fish was not so easily shaken off. "There's still the matter of burglary, assault, and kidnapping— serious crimes that must be fully investigated. I'd like you to come down to the police department tomorrow to make a formal statement and give a blood sample, so that we can compare with the drug used on your wife. We'll expect you at eight a.m."

"Certainly, Detective. Although as I told you, I won't be much help identifying my attacker." Thomas wasted no time in closing the door behind them.

Barry and Melinda walked in silence to their vehicle. Before starting the engine, Barry turned to Melinda. "Well done in there! You got him to open up and now we have something to go on. We make a good team, don't we?"

Melinda frowned, deep in her own thoughts. "Thomas isn't telling us everything, sir. I don't think he had a hand in his wife's death, but he is up to something. And if that manuscript is so explosive, wouldn't he have made a back-up? For that matter, wouldn't Geraldine have made a back-up before she deleted it from her device?"

"Hmm. We'll have to grill him about that tomorrow. Or *you'll* have to grill him. Catch more flies with honey than vinegar, eh? But let's celebrate the progress we've made so far. How about a drink?"

"I don't think so, sir. My mother's expecting me

home and she'll have a meal ready." This was not exactly true. Her mother preferred to eat early and would already be installed in front of the television for the evening. Melinda knew that it might have been wiser professionally for her to accept Barry's invitation, but she wanted to write up her notes and prepare for tomorrow's confrontation with Thomas.

Plus, her anger at Barry's bullying interrogation technique had not completely dissipated. She needed some distance.

Chapter 17

Diana watched as the detectives' vehicle pulled away from the Harmon residence. The living room light was extinguished before she could get out of her car. She hurried to the front door. Thomas was at home, and she didn't want him to use the excuse of an early night to prevent her entry. She held her finger on the doorbell for five seconds, waited for thirty more, then repeated the sequence. No response. Considering what to do next, her eye lighted on the small white box next to the garage door. A lifelong city apartment dweller with no experience of overhead garage doors or automatic garage door openers, Diana remembered Geraldine's patient explanation that in case the remote opener failed, a four-digit code entered on the keypad hidden in the box would open the door.

She walked over to the box and lifted the lid. What code would Geraldine have chosen? Nothing so mundane as her birthday. Perhaps Thomas had selected the code, in which case she had no idea what it might be. Making a wild guess, she tapped in Dickens' birth year: 1812. Nothing happened. She could hardly stand here all night entering random number sequences. She decided to give it one more try: 1870, the year of Dickens' death. The door rattled up, and she was confronted with the dim outline of Thomas's BMW. She dashed past the car to the connecting door to the kitchen, hoping Thomas had not locked it. He hadn't. She made it through to the kitchen just as Thomas appeared in the doorway to the rest of the house.

"Diana! What the hell—" Thomas was dressed for bed.

"I won't take long. I need something of Geraldine's. I'm sure it's of no interest to you, or of any monetary value. I just wanted to make sure you didn't throw it out before I could have it."

"You have no right to force your way…" Thomas's face reddened in anger, and he sputtered over his words. He had never liked Diana.

"I'm not going away, Thomas. If you don't want a scene, you'd better let me come in." Diana's calm increased as her antagonist's rage mounted. After glowering at her, Thomas turned in disgust and stalked into the living room. She followed.

"Moving out?" Diana asked, surveying the bare surfaces and absence of any personal items.

"If it's any business of yours, I've decided to go back east. The house goes on the market next weekend. Now, what do you want?"

"A photograph of Geraldine and me from our Oxford days. It was in Geraldine's—*your*—bedroom. You haven't trashed it already, have you?" She suspected it was in one of the packing boxes she had seen that morning in the spare bedroom, but didn't want to reveal her discovery of the assault and abduction. If he knew she had already invaded his territory twice that day, and that it was she who called the police, he might be even more hostile.

Thomas sighed dramatically and pushed past her to the stairs. "Stay here!" he barked.

After waiting two beats, Diana ignored his order and pursued him up to the spare bedroom. Thomas scowled at her and pointed to one of the boxes. "You can try in that one. Geraldine's personal stuff is in there. The rest goes to Goodwill tomorrow."

A rush of emotion overtook Diana as she pulled back the cardboard flaps on the top of the box. Resting on top of the other contents was a coffee mug inscribed "What the Dickens?" and decorated with the author's unkempt goatee'd face. Below that lay a thick bundle of cards and letters probably from former students, and a couple of dog-eared notebooks—how Diana would have loved to spend time with them—but her prize was near the bottom. She pulled out the photograph in its substantial frame, and closed up the box, blinking away tears.

At that moment, they both heard a noise from downstairs.

"Tommy? Are you there? The garage door's open..."

Hannah! Her voice was slurred and bumping sounds suggested she was having difficulty navigating past the furniture. Thomas rushed out of the bedroom to stand at the top of the stairs. Diana left the room more slowly, clutching the photograph.

"Hannah? What in God's name are you doing here?" Thomas struck a Henry VIII pose, feet apart, hands at his hips and chest puffed out—a desperate attempt to preserve his dignity in the face of a double invasion he wasn't dressed for.

Hannah had reached the foot of the stairs and was hauling herself up by the banister rail.

"Oh, Tommy! I was so-oo worried. You gone an'

the mess in the study. I tol' the police, 'You better find him!'"

"I'm perfectly fine. There was no need to involve the police. You should leave." Thomas's voice was icy, but Hannah paid no heed. Concentrating on the climb, she was halfway up before she spotted Diana behind Thomas's shoulder.

"You—you—harlot!"

Diana failed to suppress a snicker of laughter at the archaic insult. This enraged Hannah further, and powered her up the rest of the flight.

"I'll teach you to laugh at me!" she shouted. She struck out—a wild roundhouse of a punch. Thomas stepped adroitly aside and Diana raised a hand to fend off the blow, the hand holding the photograph. Hannah's fist opened to grab the frame. For a moment the women stared into each other's eyes before Diana loosed her grip on the photograph. Hannah reeled backward, seeming to hover in the air before falling in sickening slow-motion ricochets between the banisters and the wall until ending up in a heap at the foot of the stairs.

Chapter 18

Marco had spent the afternoon moving his belongings into Cindy's spare room. He still had two weeks' grace at the halfway house, but once he'd seen the attic room with skylights and the gable-end window looking down to the bay, he wanted to be living there. He also harbored a fear that Cindy might change her mind. She'd always been straight with him, but he had been let down before by people he trusted.

A desk stood under the window, and a recliner showing signs of wear was positioned under one of the skylights.

"Yeah, that was my dad's," Cindy said. "Not very elegant but it's comfortable. I can clear off some of these shelves if you like." She indicated the bookshelves tucked beneath the sloping roof.

"No, please leave them. I don't have many books, not much stuff at all, really. Is it okay if I read them?"

"Of course! Help yourself." Cindy opened the built-in cupboards under the other slope of the roof. "There's room for your clothes, and I put some spare sheets and towels in here too. Just remember not to stand up straight while you're getting things out, or you'll knock yourself out. You're taller than me."

"It's all great. Thank you so much, Cindy. Please let me know how I can help you around the house, take the garbage out, do the dishes, anything. I'm not a bad cook, either. Just tell me how I can repay you."

Cindy laughed. "I might take you up on the cooking. I'm getting pretty tired of frozen pizza." She turned to leave, then paused. "There is something I need your help on. When you've finished unpacking come down and have a cup of coffee with me."

It didn't take long for Marco to arrange his few possessions in the space, managing to hit his head only twice. He looked around with satisfaction before descending the narrow staircase to join Cindy. She indicated a stool at the bar separating the kitchen from the rest of the living area, and poured him a mug of coffee.

"You remember Jesús, the guy at the Mission? You said someone came looking for him the other night." Cindy pushed a sugar bowl and the carton of milk toward Marco.

"Sure, but he hasn't been back to the Mission in a while."

"That's because he's in hiding." Cindy filled Marco in on the *Cofradia* and why they were pursuing Jesús, Bill and Joan's decision to conceal him in the Old School at St. Xavier's, and the link with Professor Harmon.

"You mean she was killed to suppress a manuscript?" Marco sounded doubtful. It seemed like a plot for a mass-market thriller, unlikely in their sleepy little burgh. But then he pictured Geraldine Harmon's body sprawled over her desk, and remembered the police questioning him and Aubrey. "What are the police saying about it?"

"That's the point. They're not saying anything. If they're investigating it as murder, why haven't they released a statement or appealed to the public? You know, our police department is hardly the FBI, so maybe they don't have the tools or the manpower to handle something like this. Anyway, Bill and Joan don't trust the police, and they're the experts here. They think we should expose the *Cofradia* in the media to get them to back off. At the very least it could motivate law enforcement to act. That's where you come in."

Marco listened, his skepticism receding as Cindy explained the plan to get Professor Harmon's journalist husband involved.

"He could make an emotional appeal as the victim's widower. Because you knew the professor, and you found her body, we thought you'd be the right guy to pitch the idea to him," Cindy concluded.

"Okay, I'm in. Do you think I should email him?"

"It'd be better if you made a personal approach. Are you working tonight?"

"No, I could go over right now, if you like," Marco replied. He was pleased that Bill and Joan, as well as Cindy, trusted him with this task. Three people he liked and respected had confidence in him.

"Let's eat first, and talk it through some more," said Cindy. She opened the refrigerator door and peered in. "Let's see what you can do with cheddar cheese and a few wrinkly cherry tomatoes."

****

It was gone seven p.m. when Marco dismounted from his bike outside the Harmon house. Pushing past a car parked askew, its front nearside wheel up on the sidewalk, he secured the bike in the driveway. The garage door was open and light spilled from a connecting door to the house. Marco walked past the car parked in the garage and paused at the open door. He heard muffled voices inside and was about to call out when a series of reverberating crashes propelled him forward. He dashed through a kitchen and into a large living area at the front of the house.

"Mr. Harmon? Are you—" What he saw next choked off further speech: a body lying at the foot of the staircase. Marco was dimly aware of figures at the top of the flight, but his attention was focused on the woman on the floor. Her head was tilted sideways at an odd angle, and her eyes were glazed slits looking at nothing. He took hold of her wrist to find a pulse and leaned his cheek toward her mouth to feel for breath. Hearing someone on the stairs, he looked up to see a woman dressed in black jeans and sweater descending.

"We have to call for an ambulance! Do you have a phone? I left mine in the car." The woman crouched down on the step above the body. "Is she unconscious? Oh, God, she's not—!"

Marco stood and took his phone out. As he made the emergency call, he said, "I think it's too late for an ambulance." An image of Professor Harmon sprawled over her desk flashed into his mind. This was surreal, unbelievable: Marco had discovered two dead women in the space of a couple of weeks. Two women who were connected by one man, the man *he* had come to talk to, although that conversation was unlikely to take place now.

He sensed movement and looked upward to see a figure moving back into the shadows on the landing. "Mr. Harmon? Is that you?" Then the emergency dispatch operator spoke, asking for details, and Marco needed to concentrate on the matter at hand. He didn't notice the woman in black picking up a framed photograph lying next to the body, the glass shattered into a spiderweb of cracks.

Chapter 19

As soon as he issued his invitation to Melinda to go get a drink together, Barry Fish remembered it was his night with Connor. He was relieved when she declined and didn't stop to examine the possible reasons for her reluctance to socialize with him.

Wednesday evenings and every other weekend had been the routine since his divorce six years before. At first, Barry had ached at every parting. Time spent with his son was never enough. Now that Connor was a sullen fourteen-year-old, visitation had become more of a necessary routine. Wednesday evenings deteriorated into pizza delivery and streaming a superhero movie. The weekends consisted of Barry chauffeuring Connor to his friends' houses, and were often cut short with the excuse of homework to complete before Monday. This Wednesday, though, he had made an effort and bought tickets to a basketball game.

For NCAA Division 2, the local college fielded a competitive team, and tonight's game was a grudge match against a cross-state rival. The gym was full and noisy. Barry was pleased to see Connor animated, pumping his fist and cheering every three-pointer. He'd turned his phone to vibrate mode—pointless because the ringtone would have been drowned in the crowd's din anyway. Barry was oblivious to the pulsing phone when the call came through at a particularly raucous moment in the last quarter, when the foot-stamping and shouting made the bleachers shake. He was enjoying the rare camaraderie with his son, and dreaming of camping trips together when the weather warmed up. Perhaps he'd do okay at this dad thing after all.

After the duty sergeant failed to get through to Fish, he hesitated before trying Melinda's number. She was new to the detective squad and seemed so young. The sergeant thought of his own daughter, twenty-one years old and engaged to be married. He couldn't imagine *her* dealing with dead bodies and interrogating criminals. She squealed for help if she found a spider in the bathtub. But the call from dispatch alerted him to the need to pin down the circumstances surrounding what appeared to be an accidental death. He could send uniformed officers, of course, but since the Harmon address was already a crime scene under investigation, he called the junior detective.

****

Once Melinda had installed her mother in front of the television to wait for the game show theme music, she took a plate of scrambled eggs on toast up to her room and started work. Except for the new laptop on the desk, her bedroom was unchanged since her teenage years. The tennis trophies she had won in high school still lined up on a shelf, the poster of a romantic Rhine castle on the wall, together with a world map stuck with colored pins in all the places she wanted to visit…one day. Moving home after college was supposed to be a temporary thing until she'd finished police training and was established in her law enforcement career. But her mother's decline, which started after her father's death during Melinda's freshman year, accelerated. Mrs.

Deniro rarely left the house now, preferring the company of familiar TV hosts to friends or even family.

"Mel, you've got to move out of there. It's killing you," Melinda's older sister—married, with two pre-schoolers, in Denver—told her almost weekly.

"Yeah, I know. It's not as if Mom wants to spend time with me. I just worry she'll stop eating, or stay in bed all day if I'm not around."

"You could pop in every day, or I could call her. You need to think of yourself for once."

But Julia's nagging wasn't as bad as her younger sister's occasional middle-of-the-night voicemails, usually shouted to be heard over the background noise of a bar or club. "Got a boyfriend yet? You ought to come down here and let me fix you up." Ella lived in San Diego with two other girls, all allegedly students.

Melinda finished her supper, pushed the plate aside, and fired up her laptop. She had brought the Harmon case file home to re-read in preparation for interviewing Thomas Harmon the next morning. The theft of his computer and phone suggested a link to his wife's death. Her computer and phone had also been stolen. The key seemed to be the manuscript given to Geraldine. Melinda pulled out the email printouts made for her by Elizabeth, the English department secretary, and went over them with close attention. She'd only skimmed them up to now.

In the earliest email, Geraldine had set out her case for offering the manuscript's author a position at the college:

*Michael Obrador is an accomplished journalist with articles published in Spanish and English in newspapers and magazines such as the* Houston Chronicle, *the*

Arizona Republic, Prensa Libre, *and* El Universal. *He holds degrees from Universidad Francisco Gavidia in San Salvador and the London School of Economics.*

Melinda looked through more biographical information, then slowed at the final paragraph:

*Due to the murder and disappearance of journalists and others reporting on political corruption in Central America, Obrador is currently living under cover. His need for a safe space to complete this manuscript is therefore urgent.*

Melinda exhaled slowly. Suddenly the cases— Harmon's brief disappearance earlier that day and the rifling of his study, as well as Geraldine's death—had an international and political aspect. She entered the journalist's name in the search field on her computer. The screen filled with hits. Passing over the Spanish language items, she clicked on one in English: an article by Obrador in *Foreign Affairs* magazine two years ago. It described growing unrest in El Salvador as a result of severe hurricanes and the government's inaction in addressing the damage. There was nothing more recent in English, so Melinda scrolled back to the first item in Spanish. She had taken Spanish in high school and her Spanish-English dictionary was still on the shelf above her desk. She grabbed it.

It took her a while to find Obrador's name in the text. She concentrated on translating the paragraph in which it appeared, wishing she had kept up her study of the language through college. Eventually, she was satisfied she had wrung the meaning out: Michael Obrador was dead. In May, his body had been found in a shallow grave near the Guatemala-Mexico border. The rest of the article seemed to be an analysis of the deaths of other Central American journalists over the last several years, suggesting they may have been at the hands of police or state-sponsored gangs.

Melinda was about to tackle another Spanish language article when her phone rang.

Chapter 20

The paramedics were closing the doors at the back of the ambulance when Melinda arrived. She showed them her police ID and asked for a status report.

"Dead on arrival. Broken neck and possible subdural hematoma, but the M.E. will make an official finding," the lead EMT offered. "There's three inside. They seem to agree it was an accident; she fell downstairs. By the smell of her, I'd say she was drinking, but again the M.E. will confirm."

Melinda peeked in the back but the corpse was zipped into a black body bag. She took down the crew's details and waved them off. Although the garage door was open, she decided to approach the front door. When Thomas Harmon opened it, he was fully dressed; when she had last seen him a couple of hours earlier, he'd been dressed for bed. In silence, he led her into the sitting room, where her surprise intensified at the sight of Diana LaTour, legs elegantly crossed and back straight, sitting on the sofa. A good-looking man Melinda guessed to be in his twenties was standing by the bookcase.

"Good evening," she addressed the young man. "And what is your name and reason for being here?"

"I'm Marco Johansen. I came to speak to Mr. Harmon. I got here after...I didn't see her fall. She was there"—he pointed to the bottom of the stairs—"when I came through from the kitchen."

The name and face were familiar, but Melinda could not place him. She turned to Diana.

"How about you, Ms. LaTour? What can you tell me? Let's start with whether you knew the woman who died here?" Melinda tried to keep an eye on Harmon as she questioned Diana. He frowned as if put out that she had not spoken to him first.

Diana was succinct in her identification of Hannah Peters and her description of Hannah's arrival at the house, her state of intoxication, and her fall from the top of the staircase.

"So, you were standing at the top of the stairs with Mr. Harmon. Did Ms. Peters say anything before she fell?"

Diana hesitated, and Melinda sensed Harmon shift in his seat, itching to intervene.

"She called me a harlot. She was angry at finding me with Thomas…upstairs."

Melinda's eyebrows lifted. "Oh?"

Harmon was unable to stay quiet. "Diana had come for something of Geraldine's. I had gone to fetch it from upstairs, and Diana followed me up. Hannah was drunk. She entirely misread the situation."

"Hmm." Melinda noticed that Diana's hands were folded over something in her lap. "Is that what you came for?"

Diana showed her the framed photograph, the glass crazed into a web of cracks that obscured the subject of the picture. "Yes. Hannah grabbed it from me, lost her balance, then toppled backward."

"Do you agree that's what happened, Mr. Harmon?" Melinda turned to Thomas, who suddenly appeared reluctant to speak.

"Well, I couldn't really say. I stepped out of the way when Hannah launched herself at Diana. I heard her fall rather than saw it. Such an awful sound…"

Melinda walked them through what happened next: Marco's entrance and attempt to find signs of life, Diana's descent of the staircase and request that Marco call for an ambulance. Their wait by the body for the paramedics to arrive.

"And what did you do, Mr. Harmon?"

"I, uh, I went to get dressed."

\*\*\*\*

By the time Melinda left the Harmon house, Diana had already driven off, but Marco was waiting by an erratically parked car—most likely Hannah's. He was holding a bicycle. As she approached, the thought crossed her mind that in another life she'd like to date Marco. Tall and slim, he had the high cheekbones and deep-set eyes of a male model, and his dark blond hair was pulled back into a low ponytail. But Barry Fish's attraction to Diana LaTour notwithstanding, she knew that being in the police was like being in the convent, at least as far as witnesses were concerned. What a shame.

"Um, I was wondering who'd let her daughter know?" Marco said in answer to her inquiring look.

*Oh, God*, Melinda thought. Notifying the next of kin of a loved one's death was her least favorite duty. She could call the duty sergeant and ask for uniformed patrol officers to do it, but since she had been at the scene herself, and had interviewed the deceased earlier in the day, Melinda felt a responsibility to do the notification herself. She had Hannah's address in her notebook from that previous meeting.

"Do you know her? The daughter, I mean," she

asked.

"Yeah, a little. Aubrey and I were both in Professor Harmon's Intro to Literature class."

Suddenly it clicked into place: Marco and Aubrey were the students who found Geraldine Harmon's body. Melinda was considering this coincidence when Marco interrupted her thoughts.

"Can I come with you? It might help to have someone there she knows."

Melinda was uncertain of the protocol of taking a civilian on a death notice call, but she welcomed Marco's suggestion. "Okay, but what about your bike?"

"Race you there," Marco said with a grin she couldn't help returning. She gave him the address—less than a mile away—and he pedaled off. She opened the driver's side door of Hannah's car, retrieved the keys that had been left in the ignition, as well as Hannah's overflowing purse, locked the vehicle, then set off in pursuit.

Chapter 21

In spite of getting to bed late, Melinda was already at work the next morning when Barry Fish arrived at 7:30 a.m. She had typed up the report on Hannah Peters' death and sent it to Barry's computer for him to review.

"Wow," he said when he'd read it. "This is incredible." He caught sight of Melinda's expression, and quickly amended. "I don't mean I don't believe you—it's just all the coincidences!"

"At the police academy we were told 'a coincidence is just an explanation waiting to happen,' " Melinda said a little defensively.

"Yeah, but what *is* the explanation? Maybe we can get some clue from Thomas Harmon. Isn't he due here in a few minutes?"

"Yes. I've arranged for the blood draw. I think we should get that done first before whatever drug he was given yesterday is untraceable in his system. Then, well, I've done some research and have a line of questions I'd like to ask." Yesterday, Barry had been willing to hand Thomas's interrogation over to her, but she suspected he might want to take control again after Hannah's death.

"Oh?" Fish paused to consider. "Okay, you go ahead. I'll just be a looming presence—you know, 'bad cop' to your 'good cop.' I'll jump in if I need to."

The front desk officer called to say Thomas Harmon had arrived. Melinda left to escort him to the police

172

medic who would take a blood sample for the Medical Examiner to analyze and compare with the Angel's Trumpet extract found in Geraldine's body.

Barry Fish had turned on the recording equipment before Melinda and Thomas joined him in the interrogation room. This time, in contrast to Diana's interview, Fish did not apologize for the spartan accommodations, he just indicated the metal chair bolted to the floor in which Thomas was to sit, and then went to lean against the wall next to the closed door.

Melinda sat down opposite Thomas and opened her file. She looked down at the contents in silence until the interviewee started shuffling in his seat.

"Would you like a glass of water?" she asked him. He shook his head no with a touch of impatience. After a few more seconds, Melinda cleared her throat and began.

"We are recording this interview, Mr. Harmon. Is that okay?" He shrugged. "For the record, Mr. Harmon has indicated his assent to the recording," Melinda continued in an even tone. Thomas looked like he might protest, but then thought better of it.

"Michael Obrador." Melinda waited a beat after announcing the name. "Who is he?"

Thomas sighed. "He's a journalist my wife met a while ago. She was pretty impressed with him, I believe."

"Have you tried to contact him?"

"Me? No! Why should I?"

"So when we access your emails from your internet service provider, we won't find any communications from you to him or vice versa?"

Thomas was beginning to splutter. "Why on earth

would you access my emails? Am I under arrest? Don't you need a search warrant?"

"Mr. Harmon, we are investigating the suspicious circumstances surrounding your wife's death. I'm hoping you can help us. Michael Obrador is the author of a manuscript. People seeking that manuscript may be involved in your wife's death. Her laptop and phone were taken, we think, in the belief that the manuscript or communications about the manuscript were on those devices. Your computer and phone were taken too, maybe for the same reason. So any information you have about that manuscript and its author is relevant to the multiple crimes we are now investigating."

From his position against the wall and out of Thomas Harmon's sightline, Barry Fish gave Melinda an encouraging smile.

"I reached out to Obrador after my wife died. I have not heard back from him." Harmon spoke in a slow pedantic voice as if addressing a stupid person.

"That's because he was murdered." Melinda watched Harmon's eyes widen and his neck convulse with a swallow. "Do you have a copy of that manuscript on your computer?"

"Uh…yes," The admission slithered out between Harmon's barely parted lips. His confidence seemed to have deserted him. Melinda was quick to take advantage with a string of questions that elicited how he had obtained the copy, how much of it he had read, and what the subject matter was.

"So, based on your understanding of the content, who would have an interest in suppressing it?" Melinda asked.

"Any number of corrupt politicians in Central

America! I couldn't say who: Obrador used pseudonyms." Harmon looked like he was about to explain the long word to Melinda, so she continued without giving him the opportunity.

"Does Obrador explain how these politicians operate? Who would they use to suppress the truth about their activities?"

He thought about the question. It might have been the first time he considered the negative personal consequences of appropriating the manuscript.

"There's an organization he refers to: the *Cofradia*. It means brotherhood or fraternity, but from the context, I think it's a group of enforcers, a kind of secret police force. Their methods are violent."

"Do their methods involve drugging people?"

Harmon looked down at his clasped hands. The knuckles were white. "Yes."

The rest of the interview flowed quickly. No, he had not backed up the manuscript to another device. No, he had not included Obrador's name in the article proposal he had sent out to national news magazines. Yes, the man who abducted him may have had a Hispanic accent, but he could add nothing more to the description he'd given the day before.

Barry did not try to hide his excitement after a chastened Thomas Harmon left the interrogation room.

"This is big! We need to get the FBI involved. Maybe the CIA. A foreign criminal enforcement gang operating on US soil—it's huge!"

"We should tell the captain," Melinda suggested.

"Yes. Good job, by the way. You handled that well." Barry was already on his way out the door.

The captain, however, was unimpressed.

"This is just a string of assumptions. You have no evidence. A husband and wife have their computers stolen. Computers get stolen all the time. You can't drag in the FBI on the basis that the draft of an international thriller novel happened to be on the stolen devices."

"But the wife is dead, and the husband was kidnapped."

"The autopsy report said the wife's death was the result of a drug interaction, and the kidnap victim—" the captain put air quotes around the word "—was found a few hours later in a confused state. He can't give you a description of the kidnapper—*if* there was one. I'm not risking the reputation of this department by calling in the Feds on second-rate fiction."

Barry stared long and hard at his superior officer. Melinda, at his side, almost whimpered with frustration. The captain busied himself straightening a piece of paper on his desk.

"Anyway, what's happening with the bicycle theft inquiry? Any results yet?"

\*\*\*\*

Aubrey's Aunt Kathy arrived about noon. Although there were only three years between the sisters, Kathy was a generation older than Hannah in outlook. Her boys were grown and gone, with children of their own on whom Kathy doted. She taught elementary school and treated everyone as if they were in second grade. That was fine when Aubrey *was* in second grade and spent two weeks in the summer at her aunt's house in a small town a few hours away, enjoying regular meals and bedtimes, and trailing after her older cousins. Summer vacations at Aunt Kathy's ended with Hannah's divorce when Aubrey was eleven. After that, she was shipped off every July to San Diego, where her father now lived with Jade, his new wife. Jade was twenty-five and did not relish babysitting a step-daughter. As Aubrey resented everything about her father's lifestyle, the visits were not a success.

Within an hour of Kathy's arrival, the golden memory of long-ago summers at her place was tarnished. Kathy invaded Aubrey's room without knocking and began picking up discarded clothing, tut-tutting at the disarray.

"Come on, Aubrey. You'll feel better after a shower. What on earth is this?" She picked up a dirty coffee mug with the remains of a doobie sitting in the dregs. "Have you been *smoking*? Oh, Aubrey, sweetie!" Kathy folded her niece into a hug, ignoring the stiffness with which the girl held her body. "It's going to be okay. I called your dad, and he's booking a flight to San Diego for you next week, after the funeral. Won't it be fun to live in sunny California? And to be with your little half-sisters?" Jade had produced twin girls eighteen months earlier, a welcome excuse to stop the month-long summer visitation.

Aubrey broke away from her aunt's embrace. "I'm not going to San Diego. I'm staying here. All my friends are here. I'm in school here. I have a job—" At the thought of Mr. Karapoulas and the Mermaid's Closet, she choked up. Strange that this was the first time she had cried since Marco and the policewoman told her the night before that her mother was dead. She hadn't taken it in, she thought now—how her life could be devastated in a second, everything she took for granted thrown up in the air.

Kathy continued talking as if she hadn't heard

Aubrey. "Your dad is really looking forward to seeing you. And…Jade, is it? She's looking forward to it too. It'll be lovely, a real family for you."

Aubrey dashed away her tears, and turned on Kathy. "They're *not* my family! If he loves me so much why didn't *he* call me? I haven't spoken to him in months. Jade hates me. And where do *you* get off, arranging my life for me? You're not my mother!" She threw herself, face down, on the bed and pulled a pillow over her head. Kathy patted her heaving back for a few seconds, then stood up.

"Well, I can see you need a little quiet time. I'll be in the kitchen when you're ready to talk about it. I'll make some soup and a nice sandwich, if I can find anything in the fridge. Your mother must have liked to eat out a lot, I guess."

Aubrey left the house about twenty minutes later, mumbling something about retrieving her mom's car. After she had done this, she drove around until she found herself on campus. She snagged a parking spot, surprised at how empty the place seemed, until she remembered exam week was coming to a close. As students finished their final tests, they dispersed to spend the holidays at home. This realization provoked another wave of sobbing. Christmas had never been a big deal for Hannah and Aubrey. Last year, they had stuffed themselves with take-out Ethiopian food and done each other's nails, the polish job getting sloppier as the level in the chardonnay bottle went down.

Somewhere in the detritus on the back seat, Aubrey unearthed her Clemson knitted hat, the one she thought she'd lost at a party weeks ago. Maybe this was a gift from Beyond? Her mother looking after her in the

Afterlife? Aubrey didn't believe in eternal life, and to the best of her recollection Hannah had never told her to wrap up warm or wear a hat. She pushed her fantasy aside, and climbed out of the car.

It was raining again, disguising the wetness on Aubrey's cheeks. She jammed her hands into her pockets and headed for the cafeteria, just to be somewhere familiar. She wasn't hungry but she bought a raisin scone and a Frappuccino anyway, and sat crumbling the pastry and staring at nothing.

"Hey, how're you holding up?" Marco sat down opposite her. She hadn't noticed his approach. A surge of gratitude rose from her chest to her face and she started crying again.

"I'm…fine," she choked out.

He placed a hand over hers as it rested on the remains of the scone. "Are you going to eat that?" He smiled.

Aubrey snorted a laugh through her tears. Then she wiped her face and blew her nose on the paper napkin that came with the scone. They sat together without speaking for a while, the quiet punctuated by gusty sighs from Aubrey.

When she felt able to speak without breaking down, she said, "So what were you doing at Harmon's place last night when my mom was there? How d'you know him?"

"I had an idea for a news story I wanted to talk to him about. He's a journalist, you know."

"A story about the professor's death?"

Marco looked at her in surprise. "How d'you know that?"

"I *knew* there was something sketchy about it!" Aubrey seemed to have recovered her spirits somewhat, and Marco thought there'd be no harm in distracting her, so he explained about Jesús being on the run from the *Cofradia*, and the theory that Professor Harmon had possession of a document that exposed the gang.

"We think maybe that's why she was killed, but the police don't seem to be following it up," he concluded.

"Who's 'we'?" Aubrey asked.

"Uh, just some friends of mine." Marco saw Aubrey's face fall. "I don't mean to be all mysterious about it. It could be dangerous to get involved. I've met one of these *Cofradia* guys; they're not nice people."

Aubrey thought for a while about what Hannah had told her about Thomas's abduction, and about finding him—could it only have been yesterday afternoon?—wandering around in the rain without a jacket or shoes. Then she remembered the big pushy man who'd come into the Mermaid's Closet and shown her a photo.

"Yeah, I might have met one too." She looked at the time on her phone. "Look, I'm late for work. Walk with me to my car, and I'll tell you what I know."

Chapter 22

Hannah's death hit Diana harder than she would have expected. She thought the woman was shallow and had poor taste, but couldn't shake the image of Hannah reeling backward, mouth agape, and the sickening sound of her body crashing against the staircase as she fell. As Diana replayed the scene in her mind through the early morning hours, she asked herself if she could have done anything to save Hannah. By two a.m. Diana had convinced herself that she had caused Hannah's death by letting go of the framed photograph when Hannah grabbed it. Holding on to it tightly, might she have pulled Hannah to safety at the top of the stairs? From there it was a short mental step to wondering if she had actually pushed Hannah away, her instinctive distaste for the woman manifesting in a gesture that led to her death. At this point, Diana took one of her sleeping pills, the twelve-milligram dose, determined to think it through more rationally in the morning.

She woke after nine a.m., too late for the scheduled call to her broker in London. He would be on his way home to his family in the suburbs by now, and she never disturbed him outside office hours. After a long shower and a double espresso, she was still feeling groggy from the sedative and irritated by the departure from established routine. Last night's orgy of self-recrimination had faded to a nagging uneasiness that overlay her continuing sorrow for Geraldine's death. She had a need to *do* something.

Pacing her leased shabby-chic cottage, she searched for a way to channel her vague frustration. Reorganize the bookshelves? Sort out the spice rack in the kitchen? Her eye landed on the smashed framed photograph of her and Geraldine in their Oxford days. She had dropped it face down on the kitchen countertop when she came in the night before. Picking it up, she was again confronted with a spider web of cracked glass obscuring the two young faces. She decided to ready the image for reframing.

The thick wooden frame had come apart at one mitered corner, and the paper that covered the back was split. Diana pulled the rest of the paper off the frame, exposing the heavy card that held the photo in place against the glass and revealing a small oblong item securely taped to the card in the space inside the frame. Diana puzzled over the object for a moment. Had Geraldine hidden it there? She doubted it was Thomas, given his willingness to part with the photograph. She fetched a knife from a kitchen drawer to slice through the tape and free the thing that had been so carefully concealed. Turning it over in her hand and seeing the USB connection protruding from one end, she recognized a thumb drive. Perhaps the little device contained a clue to what had so worried Geraldine in her last days. Maybe she had even intended Diana to find it.

Diana was familiar with flash drives as a means of storing and transferring data from one device to another. Hurrying to the study where her laptop was charging, she hoped the connection would fit. She fumbled to find the port, her fingers shaking with excitement. The laptop screen revealed that the little drive contained two files. She clicked on the first of the two file icons. The data seemed to take an age to download. And then she was staring at a title page: *The Cofradia* by Michael Obrador.

Two hours later, Diana lifted her burning eyes from the screen. She had read about one third of the document without pausing. Now she needed to process its content.

*The Cofradia* told the story of a teenage boy plucked from rural poverty when his parish priest recognized his potential. He was sent to a seminary in the city to train for the priesthood. Although he understood the great privilege accorded him, the boy—referred to only by the initial J—felt lonely and out of place. The other students came from middle class backgrounds and spoke a purer Spanish than his mountain dialect. The intelligence and talent seen as exceptional in his small village were commonplace at the seminary. More troubling, he began to doubt the simple faith in which he had been raised. The complicated daily Catholic rituals he was expected to follow and the abstruse doctrinal texts set for study seemed to distance him from God. It was no wonder that when a visiting priest took a particular interest in him, J responded with shy gratitude.

The Monsignor—Diana noted that none of the characters had names, only titles, initials, or descriptive nicknames—had a close relationship with the seminary principal, and dined with him weekly. On these occasions, J had the honor of serving the meal and pouring the wine. The Monsignor often detained J to chat about his studies or ask about his village deep in the central mountains. He gave J small gifts: shampoo and soap of a better quality than the harsh-smelling bar provided by the institution, a swimsuit so that he could go to the lake with the other students on hot days. When J confessed to reservations about proceeding to ordination as a priest, the Monsignor did not chastise him but nodded thoughtfully and promised to think about an alternative path for the young man.

When the time approached for J to move on to the *collegio* to take final instruction for admission to holy orders, the Monsignor offered him a position as his secretary instead. Feeling relieved and grateful, J wrote to the village priest who had sponsored him, knowing he would share the contents of his letter with his unlettered parents. *"The Monsignor will provide me with a room in his household. I will be able to send my salary home every month."*

J's duties were light: he answered the telephone, kept the Monsignor's appointment diary, and ran various errands. There was little correspondence to deal with: the Monsignor preferred to conduct affairs face-to-face and he distrusted the internet, so there was no computer in the office. The Monsignor had some vague attachment to the Cathedral, but his primary role was as spiritual advisor to the Minister of Justice. It became clear to J that more than religious guidance was given, and to others in positions of power than the Minister. The Monsignor met with well-groomed men in sleek suits who arrived in expensive chauffeured vehicles. It was J's job to serve coffee or whiskey at these meetings. Conversation ceased when he entered the room, but sometimes resumed before the door closed fully as he left. Rather than discussion of matters of conscience, J overheard slighting references to the President or laughter at some crude sexual innuendo.

J was also required to collect documents from

government offices.

"Always insist on speaking directly to the Minister," the Monsignor warned. "Use my name."

J suspected that the thick envelopes he picked up contained money, not documents. The Monsignor, perhaps sensing J's concerns, told him these were donations "for good works." By the time J first heard the word "Cofradia" and began to understand the organization's activities, he had lost the innocence with which he had joined the Monsignor's household. His employer sat at the hub of a network of influential men who used secretive methods to accomplish their ends. The young man only realized how violent those methods were and the criminal nature of those ends when, after more than a year into his service with the Monsignor, he was sent to pick up a package from a poor part of the city.

He entered a courtyard littered with garbage. A man in a filthy singlet, his skeletal arms wrapped around his head, was crouched against a wall. J spoke the name he had been given, but the man just huddled closer to the wall. A doorway at the farther side of the courtyard was screened with a beaded curtain. As J approached, he heard chilling sounds: the thud of fist against flesh and a man's choked-off scream before the next blow landed. J called out the name again, as much to halt the activity behind the curtain as to fulfil his mission. A moment later, a giant of a man emerged, his neck as wide as his head, torso gleaming with sweat, and his ham-like fists smeared with blood. Before the beads swung back into place, J saw a figure bound to a chair, the head rolling forward onto his chest. The stink of sweat and urine, and the underlying metallic scent of blood pulsed out of the room behind. J stood frozen in place.

"Yes?" the giant inquired.

"The Monsignor sent me…" J stammered out.

The other man turned back into the room without speaking. J noted the tattoo on his swollen bicep: a cross with the word "cofradia" arranged in a semicircle around it. The beaded curtain swayed across the doorway, revealing slices of the scene beyond: the motionless figure in the chair, the pool of urine at his feet, purple bruises and bloody gashes over his naked body, his attacker behind him bent over something.

"Here," The brute returned and thrust a package toward J. The cube-shaped parcel was wrapped in plastic and criss-crossed with tape. "What you waiting for? A sample?"

J took the package and turned away, catching a pleading glance from the crumpled shape by the wall. Fighting the urge to gag, he pushed the cube into his backpack and left. He stumbled through the streets, heading for the sanctuary of the Monsignor's mansion next to the cathedral, but then remembered he was supposed to deliver the package to another address, a restaurant in a much more salubrious part of town. He realized he was carrying drugs.

****

Diana drained a glass of mineral water, still feeling the heat and smelling the foul odors of the slum described in Obrador's manuscript. She needed a break before she finished reading. Then she remembered the other file on the thumb drive. Returning to the office, she clicked on the other icon. This file contained a series of photographs, all of men and each captioned with a name. Some were official portraits, but others were clandestine snaps of a figure at a café table or lounging against a car. She clicked on the first to enlarge it to fill the screen, and gasped in surprise: it was the young man she had seen at St. Xavier's the week before when she had gone to mass with Geraldine's parents, the man who said Michael was dead. She clicked quickly through the others, seeing no names or faces she recognized. One was an elderly priest, dressed in a purple cassock with a heavy gold cross hanging on his chest: Monsignor Pedro Anguirrez de Pera. Diana understood that the photos provided a key to the coded identities in the manuscript. The two files together proved the story was not a mere piece of thriller fiction, but an exposé of organized crime and corruption. She had to find the man in the first photograph: Jesús Caron, otherwise known as J, the source of the story.

Diana stuffed the laptop with the thumb drive still protruding from it into her briefcase, and grabbed a coat. She headed for the church knowing it was unlikely that Caron would be there on a weekday afternoon, but planning to track down the priest. Father Odell might know where the young man lived. She was crackling with energy at the thought that she was getting close to unraveling the mystery of Geraldine's death. At first, Diana had assumed that Thomas was the root of Geraldine's anxieties. The attack on him and his brief kidnapping had undermined that belief, and now she understood that both Harmons were probably the targets of something much larger, an international conspiracy to silence a crusading journalist and suppress his investigation. The realization didn't make her feel any warmer toward Thomas—he was fundamentally selfish and untrustworthy—but he was irrelevant now to her search for the truth.

The church was locked and in darkness. Diana looked across the gardens that separated the building from the house next door which she guessed housed church offices. In the gloom of the winter afternoon, she spotted a slight figure walking briskly toward the rear of the green space: a woman in jeans, rain jacket and baseball cap, carrying a grocery bag. On the chance she might be a church employee or volunteer, Diana followed her to a ramshackle edifice at the back of the gardens. Most of the windows were boarded up, and a chain was threaded through the handles of the double doors. The woman unwound the chain and entered. Intrigued, Diana trailed her.

The door creaked as Diana entered the Old School. The silence that greeted her seemed unnatural. After all, someone had gone into the building not ten seconds before. There should be sounds of movement.

"Hello? Anyone there?" Diana called out.

After a few more seconds of silence an interior door opened and the woman she had seen in the gardens appeared. She had a pleasant, sun-weathered face and was in her thirties. Before the woman could close the door behind her, Diana spotted another figure in the background.

"Jesús Caron." It was a statement, not a question. Diana could not say how she knew the person in the shadows was J, but the thought occurred to her with the clarity of absolute conviction, and she spoke it without thinking. She smiled as he stepped forward into the light.

Chapter 23

At the first opportunity, after Cindy had persuaded Diana of the need for secrecy and to leave without calling attention to herself, she called Bill. She described how Diana LaTour had followed her into the Old School, and how she had identified Jesús from Michael Obrador's manuscript.

Bill remained silent, whether in shock, deep thought, or disapproval, Cindy could not tell.

"Look, I'm really sorry," she continued. "I should have been more careful to make sure I wasn't followed, but I think Diana's a good person, and at least we know what the document is now. It's the manuscript of a book Obrador wrote to expose the *Cofradia* and gave to Geraldine Harmon for safekeeping."

Bill sounded tetchy. "Yes, yes, but my first concern is Jesús' safety. If Diana could find him so easily, so can the *Cofradia*. We have to move him to somewhere more secure before word spreads further."

Cindy felt chagrined that her excitement at finding concrete evidence of the *Cofradia*'s evil doings had overshadowed thoughts of Jesús. And Bill didn't know everything yet. Before she left home to bring supplies to the Old School, Marco had told her about his conversation with Aubrey.

"I'm afraid word has already spread," she admitted. Then she described how Marco had told Aubrey about

Jesús and who he was hiding from. "It's my fault. I didn't tell Marco how important it was to keep Jesús' existence and location secret."

Bill sighed. "Well, I suppose it can't be helped. We need to get together and sort out some damage control. I'd like to meet Diana too and take a look at this document."

"Can you and Joan come over to my house? Marco's already there, and I have Diana's phone number. Half an hour?"

Bill agreed and noted down Cindy's address. Cindy disconnected, then phoned Diana. Although she felt guilty that her carelessness had allowed Jesús' hiding place to be discovered, she also sensed that Diana would be an important ally. Cindy had been impressed at how Diana had immediately grasped the significance of the manuscript and its accompanying photo array. Speaking in Spanish and in just a few minutes, Diana seemed to have forged a better connection to Jesús than Cindy had been able to achieve with her stumbling tourist phrases. She was also Geraldine Harmon's closest friend, and unraveling the circumstances of her death was a consuming mission for her. Cindy felt a momentary pang of jealousy for Geraldine. She wished she had a friend who would go to bat for her like that. Yes, Diana was impressive. And attractive too.

With Bill's grudging consent, Marco had invited Aubrey to join them at Cindy's place after she got off work at the Mermaid's Closet. She sat, eyes wide in uncharacteristic silence, like a child allowed to stay up past bedtime for an adult party.

Bill took the lead. He related for those new to the group what Jesús had told him about working in secret with Michael to record as much as he could remember of the *Cofradia*'s activities and connections. After that, Jesús had escaped, joining one of the immigrant caravans making their way north to the US border. Michael had well understood the risk to them both, and hoped to minimize it by writing the story as a novel and entrusting it to an American for safekeeping until he could find the right platform for publication. The *Cofradia* found him first. Before he was killed, he was able to get a garbled message to Jesús that "Gerry has the document."

"We have to assume the *Cofradia* somehow intercepted the message and succeeded in reaching Geraldine Harmon before Jesús could find her. I doubt they meant to kill her—the murder of a US citizen would attract too much attention—they just wanted to get hold of all copies of the manuscript and dispose of Jesús, the witness against the *Cofradia*. Killing a homeless illegal immigrant wouldn't be a problem for them." Bill looked around the group, inviting comments or questions.

Marco jumped in. "So is the plan still to get Professor Harmon's husband to write up the story for the media and frighten the *Cofradia* off?"

Diana let out a derisive sound. "Thomas Harmon couldn't get a story published in the mainstream press even if he paid for space. He hasn't written anything worthwhile in years."

Joan became defensive. "Do you have a better idea? And don't say we should go to the police, because they've shown their incompetence already. They've done nothing to catch Professor Harmon's killers."

"But it's still unclear that she was even murdered," Cindy commented. "The death's been reported as 'sudden and unexpected.' "

Diana and Marco started speaking at the same time. Bill held up his hands for silence. "Look, the immediate issue is Jesús' safety. We can talk about how best to publish Michael's manuscript later. We need to get him into hiding somewhere more secure."

"He can come stay at my house." Aubrey spoke up for the first time. "There's plenty of room."

Everyone turned to look at her.

"What? Why not? I'm on my own there now, and I don't expect any visitors. I could do with the company." She smirked at Marco.

There was a mutter of vague dissent, given voice by Cindy. "Aubrey, you've just lost your mother. I'm not sure you should take on this responsibility right now."

"And you're very young," Bill added. "I wish Joan and I could take him in, but we live in a senior living community. Everyone's always popping in and out. I don't think it would be secure."

"I'll take him." Diana spoke with her usual authority, a woman used to seizing command. Bill, however, was of an earlier generation, and resisted the newcomer's intervention.

"I'm not sure that would be wise. You're too closely identified with Professor Harmon and may already be under surveillance by the *Cofradia*. That's why your arrival at the Old School has put Jesús in danger."

Diana reddened, about to defend herself.

"Please, let's not argue," Marco interrupted. His months of group therapy had made him adept at diverting conflict. "What we need is a place that has no association with the Harmons, or with the folks—" he waved a hand around the room—"who have been supporting Jesús in hiding so far." He looked at Aubrey, and then across to

Cindy. It would be better if the solution was proposed by her. She took the hint.

"Well, I suppose that does suggest Aubrey, but—"

"Yeah!" Aubrey pumped her fist in the air in triumph. "And I've got a fridge full of food my aunty left. It'll be great!"

The discussion meandered on, but Marco's logic won the day. Before the group broke up, they had settled on a plan to move Jesús to Aubrey's house early the next morning. Cindy would park her truck in the alley behind Old School with the cover of coming to do some landscaping work on the property.

After everyone left, Marco washed the coffee cups while Cindy dried.

"I hope we're doing the right thing," Cindy said. "That kid is awfully young. I don't think she understands what's at stake here."

"I'll keep an eye on her. I have an excuse to visit because I already know her," Marco replied. "Aubrey's okay, just a bit immature. I think she needs this. It'll work out."

"I hope you're right.

****

"Accidental death," Barry Fish said in disgust as he slapped the Medical Examiner's report on Hannah Peters' autopsy down onto the Ops Center table. "Nothing to associate this with Geraldine Harmon's death."

"Shouldn't we be looking for the man who broke into his house and kidnapped him? The Central American connection?" Melinda had tried to do more research on Michael Obrador since the Harmon interview but was hampered by her lack of Spanish and the American media's general disinterest in other countries' problems. Obrador was just one of several crusading journalists murdered in the last year in Central America. None of their killers had been identified or held to account.

Fish sighed. "You're right, but we simply don't have the resources for that kind of investigation. The captain questions my expenses when I drive out of the county to interview a witness—'Couldn't you do it by phone?' " he mimicked the captain's high-pitched whine—"And you saw how he went apoplectic when I mentioned the FBI. No, I think we've hit a dead end with this." He waved a hand at the names and information scrawled on the whiteboard. "Geraldine Harmon died of a random drug interaction, Thomas Harmon can't—or won't—identify his assailant, and there's no forensic evidence. So we're left with a case of laptop and phone theft, and no leads. The perp is probably back in Mexico by now."

Melinda nodded. She shared Barry's frustration. She also worried that her temporary stint in the detective squad was coming to an end. She enjoyed the work and got along okay with Barry. He was an old-school cop, and sometimes oblivious to her Gen Z sensitivities, but she knew she could learn a lot from him if only she could stay in the squad. There was one bright spot: if the case was winding down, she was free to pursue a friendship with Marco because he would no longer be a witness in an active case. She thought about cheering Barry up with the suggestion that Diana LaTour might not be off-limits now too, but then she decided to let him work that out for himself.

"So, shall I clean this up?" Melinda picked up the dry-erase eraser.

"Suppose so," Fish replied with a sigh. "Where's that list of stolen bikes? We'd better get back to that before the captain throws another fit."

\*\*\*\*

Aubrey liked having Jesús as a housemate. It was nice to get home from work in the evening to find the dishes done and the living room picked up. Jesús had also worked out how to use the washing machine, which was more than Aubrey had ever managed. Plus, Jeremy adored him. The little dog, starved of attention before, trailed Jesús from room to room, never taking his liquid brown eyes off this godlike creature who fed him regularly and never left the house. Jesús wasn't much of a cook, but as he liked pizza as much as Aubrey did, that wasn't a problem. In exchange, she was helping him with his English. In the evening they watched TV together like an old married couple. The only hard thing was not telling Mr. Karapoulas about her new living arrangement. Mr. K had been so sweet after her mom died. He seemed pleased that her spirits had improved in the last couple of days, and she was disappointed that she couldn't explain why.

Aubrey knew it was too good to last, just a temporary hiatus before "real life" began again. In the New Year, she'd have to make some decisions about school, the house, what to do with Hannah's things, how to respond to her dad's persistent invitations to San Diego. Her Future with a capital F. For now, she was content to stay cocooned with Jesús. She wasn't attracted to him—she was still crazy about Marco—but Jesús was easy to be with, and, between him and the Mermaid's Closet, her life had a shape and purpose that was missing before.

Chapter 24

Dave drove the first three hundred miles powered by rage.

"How the fuck could she? The lying bitch! She wants a divorce? She's found someone else? Fucking unbelievable! And just before Christmas, too!" After all he had done for her, the long days on the road, sleeping in the cab, greasy food in truck stops, no drinking, no sex. Well, not much. When he'd strayed, it had meant nothing, one-night stands, while she had been shacking up for months behind his back with—and this was the hardest thing to swallow—little Emma's soccer coach! Wasn't there some code of ethics that barred coaches from screwing parents of team members? There should be.

By the time he pulled into the distribution center to unload, his anger had reduced to a low boil, and he was plotting a revenge that consisted of having sex with every woman who crossed his path. He thought about the scrawny waitress at the all-night diner up the street but remembered that her shift ended at three p.m. and she would have already left work. It would have to be Hannah. She was past her sell-by date but willing, and that was the important thing. But *would* she be willing after he had ignored all her calls and texts? And after the Facebook smear operation Joanne had engineered? He'd find some excuse—she must have mis-dialed his phone number; he never got the messages; he wasn't even on Facebook, didn't know anything about that awful post.

He made a detour to a gas station for a bunch of forlorn-looking chrysanthemums before setting out to find Hannah's house. He couldn't remember the address but had a feeling for the location, and a walk would do him good after all that fuming on the drive. He probably should call first, but Joanne had deleted Hannah's contact details and call history from his phone. Arriving unannounced might work in his favor, too—make him look eager and innocent, rather than randy and indiscriminate.

****

Melinda was due for firearms training that morning. She didn't care for it, her least favorite course at the Academy. She couldn't help flinching and closing her eyes at the last second as she pulled the trigger. Her shots scattered across the target, rarely hitting the kill spot. But she knew she had to fulfill all requirements if she wanted a chance to maintain her status as a detective.

When she arrived back at the Department, she met Barry on his way out.

"I get Christmas Eve with my kid," he explained. "There's nothing going on here. You should take the rest of the day off too. I'll see you next week. Merry Christmas!"

Melinda double-checked with the duty officer. He echoed Barry's encouragement to go home, so she left without taking the time to go to her desk. Her younger sister Ella would arrive late in the day to spend Christmas week. Ella had hinted she might even stay longer, might look into transferring to the local college and live at home for a while. Melinda knew better than to rely on this possibility, but just the anticipation of seeing her baby girl had brightened her mother's spirits and energized her to go grocery shopping. Melinda could now seize the opportunity to do some belated Christmas shopping of her own.

Although it was not in the town's main retail area, Melinda drove down the hill to the Mermaid's Closet. Maybe she'd find some earrings for Ella, or a pretty photo frame for her mom. In truth, she wanted to check on Aubrey. The girl was a prickly mix of vulnerability and hostility. The night when Melinda and Marco had gone to tell her of her mother's death, Aubrey had turned away and stared at the wall, only meeting their looks of concern when she had knitted her brows into a frown and hunched her shoulders forward as if to protect a tender spot in her chest. After they had extracted her aunt's name and phone number and a promise that Aubrey would call her for support, she had ushered them out of the house, dry-eyed.

The shop was in darkness, a "closed" sign hanging in the door—strange, on one of the busiest sales days of the year. Melinda got back in her car and returned to downtown, but her heart was no longer in Christmas shopping. She checked her phone for Aubrey's home address.

****

Mr. K's wife had an appointment in Seattle for some new experimental treatment, so he had closed the shop and given Aubrey the day off. He'd told her she could take the decorations they had used to brighten up the shop window for the holidays, so she and Jesús had spent a couple of happy hours stringing multicolored lights around the living room and spraying fake snow on the windows. With her employee discount, Aubrey had bought a set of crèche figures for Jesús, which moved him to tears. Embarrassed, Aubrey sought to distract him by teaching him the only Christmas carols she knew: "Santa Claus is Coming to Town," "Frosty the Snowman," and the rude version of "Jingle Bells." This led to watching a comic Christmas movie on the TV. Although he laughed in all the right places, the movie left Jesús sad. He tried to explain in his expanding but still limited English.

"Buddy like me. Not know how to be in the world all alone."

"Hey, you're not alone. There's me and Cindy and Marco, and those old people, and the snotty woman with great hair," Aubrey assured him. She wondered if he'd feel better if they started making out, but decided against it. He was almost a priest, after all. "Let's order Mexican food tonight for a change. You can pick. I'll find the menu on my phone." That seemed to cheer him up.

****

Dave had some difficulty finding Hannah's house. Fog had moved in from the water, curling around the streetlights and parked cars like a living thing, making strange shapes out of the bushes and trees that lined the streets. He was glad when he recognized Hannah's car in the driveway and saw the multicolored lights blinking from behind the curtains in the front room. She was home and could hardly refuse to let him in on a night like this—Christmas Eve, too.

He rang the bell, then stepped back, holding the chrysanthemums out in front of him like a bride. Aubrey, expecting a food delivery, opened the door wide, light spilling out from the hallway behind her. She gawped at

Dave.

"Hi, Amber! Merry Christmas!" Dave summoned his most winning smile, hiding his frustration that it was the sullen daughter rather than the lascivious mother who answered the doorbell. "I'm here to see Hannah."

Aubrey stared for a moment. "Well, you can't." She began to close the door.

"Hey, wait a minute! I know she's here. That's her car. I've come a long way to see her. And I brought these," he said, thrusting the limp bouquet at the girl. His smile became fixed, more like a grimace.

"Nope, not here."

The fury he'd felt earlier came flooding back. He lunged forward, impeding her efforts to close the door. "I'll wait, then," he snarled.

Aubrey opened her mouth and let out, not a ladylike shriek but a bellow of rage. Dave raised his hand—still clutching the flowers—as if to strike her. A thin, dark-haired man erupted from the room on the left of the hallway, and rushed to interpose himself between Aubrey and Dave. Dave was incensed now. All the humiliation he had suffered at the hands of women—Joanne, Hannah, Audrey/Amber/Aubrey, all the slutty truck-stop waitresses who led him on and then refused to put out, the nicely dressed depot clerks to whom he was invisible—churned and roiled into a need to take revenge, even if it was only on this skinny male specimen standing in his way. He launched himself at Jesús, but before he made contact the younger man stumbled backward over something, taking Aubrey down with him. Jeremy, Jesús' faithful shadow, finding himself under two falling bodies, let out an affronted bark. At the same moment an explosion of red-hot pain shot through the back of Dave's neck. A second shot hit him in the upper back, but he didn't feel it. Dave was dead before he hit the floor.

There was a second of echoing silence, then Jesús took in a breath. "*Abajo!*" He held Aubrey's arm to try and keep her down, but the dog was squirming underneath her. Aubrey raised her head slowly to look outside. There was another bang-bang of gunfire, but not as deafening as the first shots. She saw, beyond Dave's body on the threshold, a black heap on the path from the street. The mist shrouded another figure in the roadway itself, half-crouched with both hands extended at eye level and holding a gun.

"Police! Don't move!"

****

Barry Fish caught the request for backup with the ominous detail "officer-involved shooting" on his car radio as he left his ex-wife's house. The afternoon had been enjoyable. Connor was ecstatic over the new phone Barry gave him for Christmas. His ex had texted him the preferred specifications. She in turn seemed to appreciate the security camera he set up for her, enough anyway to invite him to dinner on Christmas Day. He'd have to put up with his ex-in-laws, but he was willing to pay that price.

He was at first inclined to ignore the alert. He was off-duty until Monday, after all, and officer-involved shootings always resulted in a shitshow: the media bleating about police reform and the union braying about "blue lives matter." In the middle would be some newbie cop who had reacted out of panic and now wanted to turn the gun on himself. But the address mentioned was in a residential area close by, and he knew backup would be thin on the ground on Christmas Eve. Still feeling the afterglow of family warmth, he turned the car around and headed for the scene.

It took Barry a couple of minutes to understand that Melinda was the "officer involved." An ambulance and a patrol car had already parked on the street when he arrived. Two EMTs were crouched over a supine body on the path to the front door. He stopped to find out that this victim was alive but barely, then moved to the group standing on the porch steps. A uniformed officer stepped aside to brief him, revealing another body splayed across the threshold of the house.

"Looks like *that* guy,"—indicating the man being worked on by the EMTs—"shot *this* guy in the back. Two bullets. He's dead," the officer added unnecessarily. "Then Detective Deniro shot *that* guy from the street."

Barry stared at the officer in surprise. "What? Where's Deniro?"

"She's over there, sitting in her car. I secured her weapon." The cop showed Barry the evidence bag he was holding.

"IDs?" Fish barked, trying to make sense of it all.

"Yeah, we were just trying to sort all that out," he said, turning to his partner, who was talking to a young man and woman huddled together in the doorway. Somewhere inside, a dog yipped without let-up.

"Okay," Barry replied. "I'll go sit with Melinda."

He squeezed into the passenger seat of Melinda's Ford Focus and looked across at the young woman he had come to respect as a colleague. She was staring forward, gripping the steering wheel. "Take some deep breaths, it's going to be okay." Still in the dark about what had happened, Barry understood the need to be patient.

Melinda followed his instructions. The first inhalations shuddered, but soon she was breathing more steadily and was able to relax her hold on the wheel. "Is he dead, the one I shot?"

"No, they're transferring him to the ambulance now." Barry looked past Melinda to see what was happening in the front yard.

"And the other one?"

"He didn't make it."

"Who is he?"

Barry shrugged. "No idea. Thought you might know."

Melinda shook her head. "I came to check on Aubrey Peters—you know, Hannah's daughter. When I arrived, I saw a man with a gun in the front yard. He was aiming at the people at the front door—Aubrey was one of them. I grabbed my gun from the glove compartment and as I got out of the car, he fired." She reached for the wheel again, reliving the moment, and needing something solid to hold onto. Barry waited. "They all fell down in a heap. I saw Aubrey's head come up, and the man aimed again. I…shot him." She turned to Fish, a look of amazement on her face. "I've never fired a gun outside the range in my life. I don't know how I managed to hit him, and it was pure chance I had my weapon with me." A bubble of hysteria that changed into sobs convulsed her.

Barry considered whether to extend an arm around her and utter the platitudes that ran through his brain—*That's what we're trained for. You did your duty. You saved lives.* He sensed at this moment she wouldn't thank him for any of those, so he sat still until she swiped the tears off her cheeks and sniffed hard. "Ready? We need to take some witness statements."

Melinda gave a firm nod. "Ready."

Chapter 25

After Christmas, the weather changed. Cold air coming out of Canada replaced the wet, windy El Niño pattern from the Pacific. The New Year began with one of those rare jewel-like Northwest winter days, the islands to the west and the mountains to the east etched sharply against a blue sky. The group standing at the end of the dock was muffled in scarves, warm coats, and gloves, shoulders hunched against the cold.

Aubrey stood in the middle, facing the water and holding the urn containing Hannah's ashes. Flanking her on one side was Mr. Karapoulas, and on the other, Cindy and Diana. Marco and Melinda positioned themselves behind. Jesús and Bill and Joan were missing. They had left for New York and Washington D.C. the day before. Diana had sent Obrador's manuscript and file of photographs to a contact at a prestigious human rights law firm in London. Once the lawyer had read it, he had flown to the States. Faster than anyone thought possible, interviews with selected national media were arranged, as well as Jesús' attendance at an *in camera* meeting of a Congressional subcommittee. Jesús, transformed into a romantic hero by a good haircut and dark suit, was accompanied by Bill and Joan. They were thrilled to be invited along as interpreters and chaperones, reliving the glory days of their activism. Diana fronted the cost of the airfares.

The lawyer had even smoothed the way for an emergency asylum application on the basis that Jesús would certainly be killed if he was deported back to El Salvador. He had identified the wounded gunman, now recovering in a federal prison hospital, as *Cofradia.* Although the gunman refused to answer any questions, this identification was confirmed by the tattoo on his bicep. The Salvadoran government was attempting to extradite the man, assuring the U.S. authorities that he would face justice at home, but the State Department and the Department of Justice, now aware of the deep links between the criminal organization and senior members of that government, were not playing ball. The *Cofradia* thug had been charged with Dave's murder, a state crime, while the FBI considered what additional federal charges might be brought.

"This feels weird," Aubrey said. "I guess I should say something about my mom, but I can't think of anything."

There was a sympathetic murmur, but, except for Diana, no one present knew Hannah so they could not supply a heartfelt memory to fill the gap. Aubrey shuffled her feet and hefted the urn from one arm to the other.

Marco came to the rescue. "Tell us what color your mom reminds you of."

"Orange!" Aubrey replied promptly. "No, wait. Bright pink."

"Leopard-skin print," contributed Diana, still feeling a residue of guilt because she had disliked the dead woman.

"Sequins and Lycra!" responded Aubrey. Everyone laughed.

"She sounds fun," said Melinda, thinking of her own mother's dark moods. "Hopeful, optimistic."

"Yeah, you could say that. She was always hoping to meet Mr. Right." Aubrey was smiling now. "She pissed me off big time, but she made me laugh, too." She lifted the lid off the urn and tipped the contents over the rail into the water. The group watched the ashes form a gritty swoosh on the surface before slowly disappearing.

After more conversation, the group split up. Melinda and Marco were the first to leave. This was their second "date" after running into each other in town the day after Christmas. Over coffee, Marco had told her about his substance abuse problems and his criminal record, even about his desperate financial state.

"I want to be completely honest with you—no secrets, nothing for you to find out later and say I'm not the person you thought I was," he said.

Melinda was taken aback. Not by his addiction and its attendant issues, but by his willingness to share it all with her. Her family had always shrouded even benign facts in secrecy, reluctant to talk about feelings, hiding it all under "everything's fine."

The next night, they went for pizza. He asked her what her plans were.

"I want to be a detective," she confided. "I like solving puzzles, finding solutions. And helping people." She blushed; it sounded naïve. Before the evening was over, she had told him about her mother's depression.

"I feel responsible for her, even if I can't help her."

Marco nodded. He didn't offer pat solutions or anodyne comfort.

\*\*\*\*

Standing next to each other on the dock, Cindy and

Diana offered the perfect illustration of the adage that opposites attract. Cindy wore jeans and a plaid shirt under a worn puffy jacket. Her hair was cut short like a boy's and the only cosmetic she ever used was sunscreen. A head taller, Diana sported a tailored black overcoat and polished high-heeled boots. She was a decade older, although her flawless complexion evidenced either superb genetic heritage or expensive serums, possibly aided by plastic surgery. But they recognized each other as strong-minded, independent and resilient women. They both had a cautious streak.

"My lease runs through May," Diana told Cindy. "I can't commit to staying in the Pacific Northwest after that."

"I'd be a fish out of water in London," Cindy admitted. "Let's just see how it goes."

****

Aubrey and Mr. Karapoulas were the last to leave.

"My wife is responding well to the treatment we went to Seattle for," he told her. "I've booked us flights for Hawaii leaving on the eighth. I wondered if you'd be willing to increase your hours and do the openings and closings? Of course, your pay would go up."

"What? You mean, like I'd be store manager?" Aubrey asked, trying to imagine it.

"Exactly! But on a temporary basis. I'll be back on the fifteenth, and I very much hope my wife will be back in the shop soon, but even then we'll need your help. We can work out a schedule that works with your classes."

Aubrey hadn't thought ahead to the winter quarter, or whether she'd still be in town or in San Diego then. She stared into the water. No trace of her mother's ashes remained. "Okay, I'll do it," she said, smiling. "Yeah, it'll be great!"

\*\*\*\*

No one had mentioned Thomas Harmon, although Geraldine Harmon was never far from Diana's mind. She had driven by the house and seen the "For Sale" sign in the yard. The place looked unoccupied. Without really knowing why, she had parked and walked up the driveway and around to the back. Thomas's cherry-red sportscar was no longer in the garage. Diana peered through the kitchen window to see bare countertops—even the coffeemaking paraphernalia was missing. When she called the number on the realtor's sign, she was told the owner had moved back east and she could look over the property at her convenience. She declined and hung up.

\*\*\*\*

After two days of driving, Thomas arrived in St. Paul. He had given his brother the minimum notice, not allowing him the opportunity to find an excuse to avoid the visit. Brother James—or Jimmy, as he now preferred—was on his third wife. The only thing the brothers had in common was their taste for fast German-built automobiles. Thomas intended to stay with Jimmy until Geraldine's life insurance money came through, or the house sold, whichever happened first, and then perfect his move to the East Coast—a cottage on the Cape or a cabin in Vermont: somewhere he could reinvent himself as the reclusive writer. He was done with journalism, and with women. He had a new idea for the Great American Novel. The setting: the English Department of a small liberal arts college on the West Coast. The hero is the ruggedly handsome, fiercely talented but under-appreciated professor of twentieth century literature; his antagonist, the pompous, near-senile head of department, and father of Gwenda, the ethereally beautiful but unstable cellist with whom our hero is in love. The blurb almost wrote itself.

# Acknowledgments

This story started as a writing exercise inspired by the "six degrees of separation" theory—the idea that everyone is somehow connected to another person by no more than six other people. I wanted to develop several disparate characters and then link them by a plot. My tendency is to mystery, so naturally there's a death to start the ball rolling.

Thanks go to my writing group (Linda Lambert, Amory Peck, Lisa Dailey, and Aaron Palmer) for their perceptive critiques, fine editing, and above all for their unflagging encouragement throughout the writing process. I rely on this group for support and accountability; I could not write without them.

I am grateful for the inspiration provided by the place I live: a small college town in the Pacific Northwest. My previous novels have had an international flavor. It was a pleasant change to do my research outside my own door. And, of course, lifelong gratitude to Graham, who loves everything I write, and is an excellent proofreader.

## A word about the author…

Marian Exall is an award-winning author of mysteries and historical fiction. She grew up in England and lived in France and Belgium before emigrating to the USA, raising a family and pursuing a career as a lawyer. She now lives in the Pacific Northwest with her husband of more than fifty years and her dog Bo. Find out more at https://www.marianexall.com.

www.ingramcontent.com/pod-product-compliance
Lightning Source LLC
LaVergne TN
LVHW010054230925
821732LV00041B/1046